General de Saint Brieuc, the aging head of the family which has lived at Keralic for centuries, is devastated when his daughter is found drowned in the lake. His turbulent relations are gathered in the great house and he arranges her burial quickly – in fact with such speed that he is believed to be hiding the truth.

At Keralic the divisions amongst the family are exacerbated by the tragedy and when the house is cut off from the village by a heavy snowfall the atmosphere becomes positively electric. Before anyone can get through to them, another member of the family is found dead, and this time there is no doubt it is murder.

Commissaire Orloff is despatched from Paris to investigate the death. He is an investigator of intuition and flair, a man of dedication and high intellect, but what he finds at Keralic stretches even his ability.

This is a whodunnit in the traditional style: full of clues, suspects and red herrings, and a delightful policeman who disentangles the mystery through pure detection and to the satisfaction of all readers.

by the same author

TASTE FOR MURDER
DEADLY RETURN
SHROUD OF CANVAS
DANGEROUS REFUGE
DANGEROUS MERCHANT
THE QUEEN DIES FIRST
KILLER'S LAUGHTER
LET THE WITNESS DIE
POINT OF DEATH
WATCHER ON THE SHORE
COME BACK AND DIE
GRIP OF FEAR
THE IDENTITY TRAP
PAST TENSE
ROONEY'S GOLD

Isobel Lambot
Still Waters
Run Deadly

MACMILLAN
LONDON

First published 1987 by
MACMILLAN LONDON LIMITED
4 Little Essex Street London WC2R 3LF
and Basingstoke

Associated companies in Auckland, Delhi, Dublin, Gaborone, Hamburg, Harare, Hong Kong, Johannesburg, Kuala Lumpur, Lagos, Manzini, Melbourne, Mexico City, Nairobi, New York, Singapore and Tokyo

British Library Cataloguing in Publication Data

Lambot, Isobel
    Still waters run deadly.
    I. Title
    823'.914[F]   PR6062.A48/

    ISBN 0-333-43439-0

Typeset in Baskerville by Bookworm Typesetting, Manchester
Printed and bound by Anchor Brendon Ltd, Essex

AUTHOR'S NOTE

The author wishes to thank Prince Peter Wolkonsky for permitting her to use the great garden of Kerdalo as the setting for this novel. She also wishes to thank Countess Helene d'Andlau for her constant encouragement during the writing of the book.

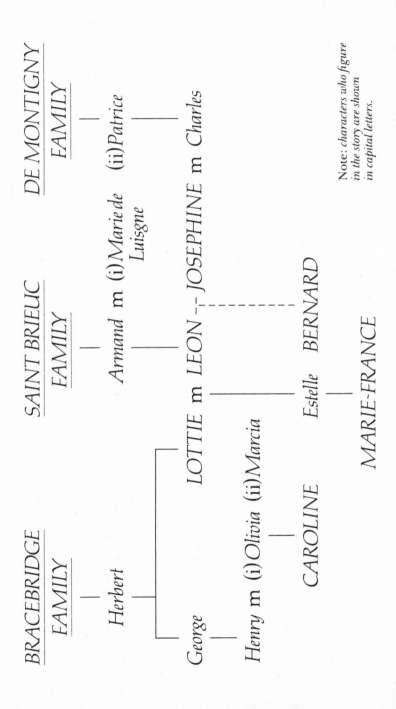

BRACEBRIDGE
FAMILY

SAINT BRIEUC
FAMILY

DE MONTIGNY
FAMILY

Herbert

Armand m (i) Marie de   (ii) Patrice
                    Luisgne

George

LOTTIE m LEON -- JOSEPHINE m Charles

Henry m (i) Olivia (ii) Marcia

Estelle   BERNARD

CAROLINE

MARIE-FRANCE

Note: characters who figure
in the story are shown
in capital letters.

Chapter 1

The scandal came at the right moment. The winter was hanging on when it should have been about to pack up its traps and go. It was nearly the end of February and the joyous hint of spring should have been filling the Breton air. Everyone was sick of the unusual cold spell – there had been snow, even, a week or two back, enough to set the old men searching their memories for when it last fell. The farmers mourned endlessly over the ruined crop of early cauliflowers, when they were not joining in the general complaints about the cost of heating. And all the time, the wind blew steadily from the north: from England, which was much colder than Brittany but whose people were rather more accustomed to it, across the unkind sea, blasting the Channel Islands on its way – more ruined crops – to roar along the Côtes-du-Nord and up the estuary, chilling the little town of Tremerrec to its mediaeval bones.

The untimely end of Estelle de Saint Brieuc gave the whole place a lift, pushing vegetables and fuel firmly into second place. It had all the makings of a juicy bit of gossip: a woman in her prime and with a dubious reputation; the fatal plunge into a lake; and, most important of all, the tragedy occurred in the old manorhouse of Keralic. The Saint Brieuc family had been around for centuries, and while they were no longer the feudal lords of Tremerrec, they were still in possession of their ancestral home on the far bank of the wide river.

Only the barest scraps of information seeped out of Keralic itself, the balance being made up by pure invention or by the indiscretions of junior policemen who were no match for the curiosity of their female relations. The town was agog to hear the result of the police enquiry. Nor was it disappointed.

7

General de Saint Brieuc pocketed his pride and admitted that his daughter had taken her own life.

Now *there* was something to chew over, recalling poor Estelle's many indiscretions, past and present, all spiced up with the spectacle of the honour of an ancient house in the dust.

'That is the trouble with these old families: rotten to the core,' said the baker's wife, a round comfortable body of generally mild views, suddenly exuding a distinct whiff of 1789. 'Not that I have anything against the General. Always the perfect gentleman.'

'More than you can say of his wife,' said her customer, picking up her half-baguette. 'Very standoffish. Always has been. Mind you, she isn't French,' she added, as if that accounted for a good deal.

The baker's assistant came into the shop with a tray of *pains au chocolat*. He was a lanky young man with hair cut into fashionable spikes.

'Madame,' he said, acknowledging the customer, and setting down his tray. He propped himself against a convenient set of shelves, ignoring a muffled roar from the hinterland of the shop, where the *patron* toiled.

'That granddaughter is a bit of a one,' he said, revealing that he had caught the tail-end of the conversation. 'Down in the bar on the quay every night, with that American *numéro*. Why doesn't she go for the local talent? She looks a bit of hot stuff, that Marie-France.'

'Following in her mother's footsteps,' said the customer, paying for her bread. 'Oh, there's Madame Quennec!'

The bakery was halfway along one side of the main square of the town, an excellent viewpoint for watching everything that went on in Tremerrec. A grey-haired woman was picking her way through the cars parked on the slippery ice-packed cobbles.

'I wonder how *she*'s feeling,' the customer went on. 'Georges is away, you know,' she added.

Two heads nodded in agreement.

'I doubt if she's all that sorry,' said the baker's wife. 'Georges was a fool to get mixed up with Estelle. That sort clings together. They don't welcome outsiders.'

8

'Not a butcher's son, anyhow,' said the boy, with a wide grin.

Through the shop window, all three watched the trim figure of Odile Quennec mount the steps of the cathedral porch and disappear through the heavy oak door.

'The funeral is at eleven,' said the baker's assistant. 'Very particular she is,' he added, acknowledging that Madame Quennec had an official capacity as sacristan.

As if in agreement, a lone bell began to toll.

Inside the icy Gothic church, Madame Quennec was bustling about, checking the arrangements. She took the work seriously, determined to prove that a woman could do the job as well as any man.

She trimmed the candles round the tomb of St Ives, and put a match to a few that were unlit. The little flames united to make a cheerful glow in the gloom.

Another candle was thrust into her hand.

'Light this for me,' said a quiet sad voice.

She all but dropped the thin wax taper.

'Georges!' she said to her son. 'Oh, Georges!'

He was rather tall, and his clothes seemed to hang on him as if the flesh were shrinking. In the light of the shrine his face was grey, his thinning hair only a slightly darker shade.

'When did you come?' she said.

'Last night. Very late. Mother, I didn't know about Estelle until this morning. Why didn't you send for me?'

She raised one hand in a helpless gesture.

'What good would it have done? Besides, there was your work – your first big chance – and then, your father—' She broke off, shaking her head.

He put a hand on her arm and the grip hurt her.

'I am not going to let them get away with it, Mother.'

Overhead the sky was leaden and a piercing wind was blowing up the estuary, chilling the soul as well as the body. The wide river was a rippling sheet of dulled silver. Below the soaring arc of the bridge, a few boats were moored in the port. Beyond them the old town climbed up to the silhouette of the cathedral, its spire a pattern of dark lace. Dim tones from the belfry tolled out a diffuse and intricate half-hour.

Caroline Bracebridge shivered in her borrowed clothes, and wished herself miles away. She had no business here. The snag was that, for the moment, there was nowhere to go.

A month ago she had been glad to come here, back to the Brittany she remembered from school holidays. But that was all blue skies and sun – before her parents managed to mess up their own lives and hers – not to be compared with the grey of winter. She told herself that she should have known the memories were deceptive, that the child had not understood how the grown-ups were tearing themselves apart.

She understood well enough now. Trust her to run away from one mess and find herself in another.

She turned her back on the view to join the others, encountering a black look from one of them. She ignored it. Bernard de Montigny was a swine. Tall, elegant, even handsome in a dark fashion, and certainly the only one there who did not look dressed by courtesy of Oxfam, but nonetheless a swine.

The rest had their backs to her, black as crows in timeless mourning clothes dragged out of closets for the occasion. All except for their feet, which were clad in the rubber boots everyone wore at Keralic, the tops brushing skirts or wrinkling trouser legs. There was something endearing about those boots, robbing the small ceremony of its solemnity in their practical insistence on mud and deep wet grass.

She wished they would get on with it.

The mourners were gathered before the ancient stone Calvary, set above them on its rocks. How much tragedy had it seen, that simple stone pillar supporting the short-armed cross and the stumpy figures with their broad Breton faces? Had it witnessed any more bizarre gathering than this family, with its mixed blood, crossed loves and hates?

The three old people were at the front. Great-uncle-by-marriage Léon in the middle, stooped with infirmity, his thin white hair blowing in the cruel breeze. On his right stood his old comrade-in-arms, Colonel Clermont, upright and military, unbowed by his years. And on the left, Great-aunt Lottie, in a shapeless hat, still unmistakably English, unchanged after all the years abroad.

It was an unending source of amazement that a family so

John Bullish as the Bracebridges should have this foreign connection, that anyone so blatantly Anglo-Saxon as Lottie could have married a Frenchman.

I might have done the same thing myself, Caroline thought, as her eye travelled to Bernard de Montigny, standing watchfully to one side. Something seemed to have upset him all right, and she did not believe that it was grief. No one could pretend that he and his cousin, the late Estelle, were any sort of friends. Caroline reminded herself that she was well out of the entanglement with Bernard.

Next to him stood the small figure of the dead woman's only child. Marie-France's face was pinched with cold as she huddled in the black coat three sizes too large for her. What did *she* feel about losing her mother, when in life they had done nothing but quarrel?

The last member of the party was standing slightly apart from the rest. Josephine de Montigny, English, too, her own mother's friend and neighbour, allied to this French family by a dead marriage and the person of her son. Through all the ceremonies of the morning – at the church, the cemetery, and now at the Saint Brieuc private Calvary – it seemed to Caroline that Josephine had kept as far away as possible from Bernard.

What a bunch we are! she thought. United not even in grief but rather by respect for the decencies; held as in a web of tangled lines of blood, marriage, friendship and bitterness. It was difficult to know where the process began, to bring them together on this windswept river bank.

There were some people missing: Charles de Montigny, Uncle Léon's half-brother, for one. Was he really ill, as reported, or was he dodging his ex-wife and/or their son? She remembered that her father used to call him 'The Invisible Man'.

And there was another who should be attending his first cousin's funeral: her father, Henry Bracebridge. His absence was no surprise. That woman – Caroline could not even bring herself to think of her stepmother by name – kept him on a very short leash.

The silence was almost beyond bearing.

In the centre of the group, the old man laid aside his stick, straightened a once-erect military spine, and held out an imperious right hand. The equally old man beside him put into it a wreath. It was made of waxy white lilies, sad hothouse blooms already shrivelling in the cold. Across the middle lay a ribbon. On it a single word: Estelle.

Awkwardly, with the painful movements of the old and disabled, he laid it at the foot of the Calvary.

Making one final effort, General Léon de Saint Brieuc stood to attention for a moment. Then his wife handed him the stick and his shoulders drooped as he let it take his weight. He turned away. No one uttered a word, not even Aunt Lottie, who could be relied upon to criticise everything her husband did. Silently, she fell into step beside him as the General began to make his slow way back along the grassy track.

A sound broke the silence: a heavy gulping sob from the girl standing beside Bernard. The Colonel, more upright than his old comrade, and not needing the help of a stick, put out a hand and took Marie-France's arm, drawing her away to follow her grandparents. She stumbled along, shaken by the sudden onset of grief.

Caroline stared after her. A week ago, Marie-France and her mother had been at each other's throats. Death had put a stop to all that, and those tears seemed real enough.

A black-gloved hand slipped under her arm.

'Caroline,' a voice said, barely above a whisper. 'Walk with me.'

Josephine de Montigny, whom she had been avoiding for the past ten days, as far as it was possible for anyone to dodge a fellow guest; just as she avoided her at home, which was not easy living in the same village. But she was glad of her now.

They turned to follow the others. Out of the corner of her eye Caroline could see Bernard stiff with disapproval. It was nothing to do with him. Before last year's 'awkwardness', she had rather liked Josephine.

She gave the gloved hand a little squeeze, glancing down at the face half-concealed by an awful black hat. Aunt Lottie's revenge, that was. But it had failed, as had the rest of the outfit. Josephine was the sort who would look elegant in an

12

old sack. Caroline felt big and awkward beside her. It occurred to her that Aunt Lottie must always have had to contend with that.

It was very odd that Josephine was there at all. Bernard, yes, family lawyer and all that, as well as being the General's nephew; but his mother was by way of being the skeleton in the family cupboard.

Caroline had a shrewd idea that Josephine was feeling as much an intruder as she did herself, and not merely because they both happened to be English and a long way from home. It was by Estelle's doing that they came to be at Keralic – and Estelle had left them in the lurch.

Slowly, the little band of mourners made their way towards the house. The track wound along the side of the valley, their boots swishing through the grass. On one side the bank rose steep and wooded. On the other, through the trees came glimpses of the water that flowed down in streams and ponds to the wide river.

Now they were walking above the main lake. In spring it would be all colour, mirroring banked azaleas, and splendid trees. Now it was pewter-grey and still, inevitably drawing the passing eyes.

That was the place: Estelle's chosen exit.

Caroline suppressed a shudder, and felt a sudden tightening of the grip on her arm.

It did not bear thinking about, that plunge in the darkness into icy oblivion.

Hastily she looked across to the opposite hill, crowned with bare branches against the bitter sky.

The track gave onto the drive, curving down the slope to the ancient manorhouse, all honeyed stone and sweeping roofs broken by dormer windows, and rising above the chimneys, the square tower with its turret and weathercock.

They reached a small courtyard. In front of them, arches piercing a wall led to the grassy upper court. On either side lay two wings of buildings. The kitchen was on the right, the big door open wide. There were other entrances, but everyone always came and went this way.

There was a little confusion at the door, where the maid,

almost as old as her employers, hovered in some vague ritual of welcome, while the mourners kicked off their boots and hunted for their shoes.

'We're late,' said Lottie distinctly. 'Why are we always late?'

Her words broke the grim spell which had held them all. Time – normal time – caught up with them in a rush, pushing eternity aside along with the one they had consigned to its keeping that morning.

'Berthe says luncheon is waiting,' the high old voice piped on. 'Hurry up, all of you.'

They sat down, this ill-assorted band of mourners, in the half-heated dining room, with its high beams and towering fireplace where the hearth had been cold for as long as anyone could remember. Caroline, who, for some reason she could not fathom, felt obliged to keep an eye on that beastly Bernard, observed him glance at the piled logs to which a match was never put, and shrug himself more closely into his jacket. Proper hothouse plant he had turned into. It really was too bad of Estelle to finish herself off just now. Why could she not have done it weeks ago, at Christmas, say, when she could have caused the maximum trouble? It was not like Estelle to pass up a chance like that. She could have had the satisfaction of knowing that she had spoiled everyone's holiday, and Caroline would not have found herself pushed willy-nilly into the company of Bernard de Montigny.

There was nothing jolly about this funeral feast, no relaxation, no sense of relief that the deceased was safely under ground and life could resume its course. The thing had been done, but furtively, with not even nearest friends invited; only immediate family, and a hanger-on like herself whom chance had brought to Keralic.

It was Estelle's father's choice to do it this way. Lottie was all for putting on a brave face and inviting all the proper people. But he would not have it. General Léon de Saint Brieuc, Chevalier of the Legion of Honour, Croix de Guerre, and a host of other decorations, was bowed down beneath the shame of his only daughter's suicide.

Berthe waited at table, in her usual offhand manner. A squat body, of good solid Breton stock, with a moustache of stiff black bristles and streaky grey hair scraped back into a bun, Berthe seemed never to change. As far back as Caroline could remember, the old servant had looked the same, and that moustache the nightmare of her childhood.

'Come and give Old Berthe a big kiss, my darling,' was always the cry, as they arrived for their annual visit. Only her mother's thumb in her back had prevented her from running away, screaming.

Her mother. That was the forbidden subject. Caroline shut it out of her mind.

'You aren't eating,' Berthe commented loudly. 'It's turned very cold and there's surely worse to come, so you should have some hot food inside you. There's only a cold supper tonight.'

'It won't hurt them to starve a little,' said Lottie, looking along the table from her vantage point at the end. 'You all eat too much,' she informed the company.

It was hardly the remark of the perfect hostess, but that was Lottie, always knowing exactly what everyone should do and making no bones about telling them. Her grey eyes sharpened with satisfaction as she perceived that she had succeeded in robbing them of what little appetite they had.

Naughty old thing! thought Caroline. Turning her face to her great-aunt, slowly and deliberately she speared a whole potato and popped it into her mouth.

She was too old to be called to account for bad table manners. Lottie glared at her, while the rattle of forks on china, as the others began to eat again, proclaimed her little victory.

Lottie de Saint Brieuc stared at her reflection in the mirror of her dressing-table. What a fright she looked, with all that wild white hair and skin like an old turkey! The black dress did nothing for her, either. Not that it mattered. Nothing had, for a long time.

She was glad to be away from the others. She had left them glumly drinking coffee in the library. It was to be hoped that they would all go away very soon.

Someone tapped at the door, and entered before she had time to screech a denial.

'Grandmama,' said Marie-France.

15

'What do you want?'

The girl let the discouraging tone wash over her. 'Can we talk?'

Lottie sighed. 'If we must.'

Marie-France walked over to the window. Dim winter light fell on her dark bobbed hair and slender figure. Not a bit like her mother, thought Lottie, not a trace of the good English blood I brought into this rotten family. Estelle had taken after the Bracebridges: tall, well-built people, strong and fair-headed, decent Anglo-Saxon stock. Young Caroline could be taken for her daughter, but not this petite brunette, French to her fingertips.

'Why did you let that woman come here?'

No need to ask whom she meant.

'Your mother asked Josephine to come.'

'Why, for heaven's sake?'

'She was one of the only friends my poor Estelle had left,' said Lottie evenly.

'How could she do that to you?'

Lottie shrugged. 'I doubt if she cared a fig for my feelings, or even thought I might have any.'

Marie-France looked at her doubtfully.

'Why is Josephine still here?' she said, opting for a question that might be answered truthfully.

'She had to stay for the funeral. It was only decent.'

'Decent!' snorted Marie-France. 'Don't you mind?'

'Not particularly.'

'How can you, Grandmama? After what she did?'

Lottie smiled grimly.

'She wasn't the only one, Marie-France. It takes two to commit adultery.'

'Grandmama!'

Lottie surveyed her granddaughter calmly.

'Do I shock you? I understood you young people thought about nothing but sex. Or is it that you don't expect us old fogeys ever to have had passions?'

'But how could Grandpapa? Oh, God! It's a horrible thought. I can't bear it.'

'If I can, I don't see why you can't,' returned Lottie indifferently, turning back to her looking-glass. 'Is that all you wanted to talk about?'

'I don't want to talk about Josephine at all!' said Marie-France violently.

'You brought the subject up.'

'I didn't mean to. It just popped out. Grandmama, what am I to do?'

Through the mirror, Lottie eyed her. 'You mean about Chester? That really is a ridiculous name. It is a place, not the sort of thing you call a child.'

'It's quite common in America. I can't see anything wrong with it.'

'I suppose not. Love blinds one in every direction. But I am the wrong person to talk to about this, Marie-France. You know perfectly well what I think. You owe it to your family, if not to yourself, not to throw yourself away on a layabout. What do you imagine you would live on?'

'Chester would find a job.'

'Has he said so?' demanded Lottie, and perceived at once that she had scored a hit. 'Let me remind you that there is a little thing known as unemployment. To get a job these days one has to be able to offer something. That Chester of yours is a foreigner, which makes matters worse. What can he offer? He has set his mind on getting his feet under the table in this house.'

'He loves me!'

'Ha! He loves what you stand for: a free meal ticket. Whatever is he doing on that boat in the port, anyway? His sort are all over the place in the summer, but he has been here all the winter. And don't tell me it's because of your bright eyes.'

'Why shouldn't he stay to be near me?' Marie-France flared.

'Suit yourself. There's none so easily deceived as those who want to be. Does he own that boat?'

The girl flushed. 'It belongs to a friend,' she muttered.

Lottie let out a bark of harsh laughter.

'Of course! Your Chester is free-loading, as usual.'

Marie-France dissolved into tears.

Lottie gazed at her dispassionately for a moment, then relented.

'Look, child, I may be a cynical old woman, but I do remember what it was like to be young. You have known him only a few months, and he is just a footloose American

17

washed up here. Your grandfather and I would be failing in our duty if we did not insist on knowing something about him, about his family. We failed miserably with your mother. Now we are trying not to repeat the mistakes.'

Marie-France looked at her out of swimming eyes.

'Grandmama, why did she kill herself?'

Lottie's mouth set in a grim line.

'Your mother was her own worst enemy. She had every advantage, yet she threw it all away. She married a worthless lout, and had a breakdown when he walked out on her. She didn't even try to look after you. Just dumped you here and went off for months on end. And when she did come back she was always in such a terrible state. She was forever threatening to kill herself. Every time she was crossed. She made an attempt once, years ago. I have spent years fearing another. Now, finally, she has done it.'

Marie-France stared at her, aghast. 'How can you be so calm? You are talking about your own daughter! My mother! I can't bear to listen to you.'

She ran out of the room, slamming the door behind her.

Lottie turned back to her mirror. It showed her a ravaged face – which was all that one could expect in the circumstances.

Yet, if the agonising loving were over, so was the pain. No more quarrels, no more screaming and abuse, no more fear of violence.

'Forgive me, Estelle,' she murmured aloud. 'But it is better this way. For both of us.'

'I really don't see why it had to be done in such a hole-and-corner fashion,' said Colonel Clermont, kicking an inoffensive clod of earth out of his path as if it had put itself deliberately in his way. 'There is nothing to be ashamed of, Léon. It could have been an accident. Estelle was drunk.'

'Don't say that!' snapped the General.

'I can't see that it is as bad as insisting that she committed suicide. We all know she was hitting the bottle that night.'

The two old men, one bent, one upright, walked on in silence, down the path slippery with sodden leaves, heading away from the house, towards the grotto overlooking the river.

Suddenly, the General stopped.

'Edouard, she told me she was going to do it.'

'When?'

'That afternoon. She came into the study when I was working.'

The Colonel looked sharply at his old friend. 'And just announced it?'

'We had a quarrel. As usual. You don't know what it has been like, these past years, Edouard. We haven't seen you for so long.'

The Colonel glanced up at the sky. 'It's too cold here for my old bones, Léon. I need the sun.'

'How long is it? Must be all of twenty years. Too long, Edouard. One appreciates old friends more as the years go on.'

'There are fewer of them.'

'That's true,' sighed the General, resuming his slow steps. 'I don't think I have told you how pleased Lottie and I were when your letter arrived.'

'Was Lottie pleased?' asked the Colonel bluntly. 'I have the impression that she doesn't care for visitors.'

'She's changed. But she can't count you as an ordinary visitor. You are Estelle's godfather. I'm sorry she had to do it while you were here.'

'Look,' said the Colonel, accepting that the conversation had come full-circle. 'Are you sure she meant it? Didn't you tell me she had made these threats before?'

They were walking past the lake now, with a green slope dotted with bushes falling gently to the level of the water.

The General stopped in his tracks.

'What is that doing there?' he barked, waving his stick towards the lake.

The old friend stared round, bewildered. 'What? Where?'

'That branch over there. François was using it to prop up that camellia. The gale last week broke it nearly in two.'

The Colonel was already halfway down the slope. A sturdy branch with a forked top was lying on the grass, not far from where half of a big bush leant drunkenly askew.

'That's it! Shove it in again, there's a good fellow. Hook it with the fork and push it in as far as it will go.'

Under the General's eagle eye, Colonel Clermont worked

the prop back into position. On the bush fat buds were waiting for the sun to burst them into life.

'I don't know what is the matter with this year,' the General grumbled. 'I can't remember a winter like this. And I can't say that I like the look of that sky.'

The Colonel was staring at the water. 'Poor Estelle!' he said. 'You know, I always think of her as she was when she was little.'

'You keep those memories, Edouard,' said his friend in an old shrivelled voice. 'I wish to God I could remember her that way. But I can't. All I can see is what she had become. She was so precious. We didn't expect to have a child, getting married so late. Lottie was nearly forty. But she has always been so strong. She was strong when Estelle came home this time. We thought she had turned over a new leaf. She said she wanted to help me with my memoirs. Did I tell you I was writing a book?'

The Colonel shook his head.

'No. It should be worth reading.'

The General shrugged. 'I doubt it. Too many old soldiers have launched into print already. It's Lottie's idea. To keep me occupied now that I'm too doddery to get about much.'

'Why shouldn't you? You've been through enough campaigns.'

'Nobody will want to read about them. Estelle didn't stick at the job long. Sorting through the notes bored her. But you know my wife. She never gives up. As soon as she heard about Caroline's mother, Lottie hauled the girl over here to take Estelle's place.'

'Did Estelle mind?'

A curious expression passed over the General's face. 'If they'd been a normal mother and daughter, I would say they had cooked it up between them. But there was no knowing what went on in Estelle's head. She seemed to be pleased. It just shows you how wrong you can be. That's why I didn't take much notice of that last outburst. She always flew into a rage if she was crossed, and would threaten to do away with herself. To make us sorry. She's done that all right, this time. I keep telling myself I could have stopped her.'

* * *

20

Bernard de Montigny stared coldly across the room at his mother. They were alone in the library now, the others dispersed throughout the house on their own affairs.

'I didn't expect to find you here,' he said abruptly.

'Nor I you,' she returned coolly.

'It is my place. I am family.'

A small smile appeared momentarily on Josephine's face. Her eyes flickered to the portrait of the General which hung over the fireplace. A fine handsome man in the prime of life, nothing to do with the feeble octogenarian.

'Oh, yes, so you are.'

Bernard found himself grinding his teeth. His sharp eyes missed nothing. It was as near an admission as his mother had ever made. He pounced on it.

'I have a right to know the truth, Mother. That picture is a dead giveaway. Or is it just a coincidence? Father doesn't resemble him, his own half-brother, but I do. So who is my father? Your ex-husband or the General?'

Josephine looked at him helplessly, wishing she had escaped when she could. Being pinned down by Bernard was not pleasant. He was making a name for himself in the courts. She pitied his opponents.

But this was not a case being heard before a judge. She would not give her son satisfaction.

'Family likenesses go in strange patterns. Or maybe it is random. Look at Estelle and Caroline. The relationship is distant – second cousins, or first cousins once removed, I forget the niceties – yet they have the same general shape and colouring. Quite obviously of the same stock.'

Bernard glared at her. 'Mother, I won't be put off. I can't imagine how you and Father ever met. He hates foreigners and spends all his time at the races. As I recall, you hardly know one end of a horse from the other.'

Josephine fixed her gaze on the white marble mantelpiece, which supported a variety of interesting and valuable objects.

'I met him here,' she said. 'My father was an acquaintance of Lottie's. They arranged for me to spend the summer here, to look after Estelle in the school holidays and improve my French. Where is your father? I am surprised that he has not come.'

21

'He's not very well at the moment,' Bernard replied curtly.

Josephine nodded.

'Still on the bottle?' she enquired gently, and was pleased to see her son's quick frown. 'Poor Charles must be thoroughly pickled to have lasted so long. He must be touching seventy now.'

Bernard's frown deepened.

'Why is Caroline here?' he demanded, changing the subject.

'Oh, for goodness sake! What is the matter with you? What am I doing here? What is Caroline doing here? Can't Lottie and Léon invite whom they please to their own house? You should have enquired who was here before you decided to set foot in the place. If anyone has cause for complaint, it should be Caroline. You behaved very badly last year.'

Bernard could not meet her eyes.

'I don't like being pushed.'

Josephine stood up, happily aware that this was one of the rare occasions when she had got the better of her brilliant son.

'No one was pushing you. Caroline and her mother and I all live in the same village. It is quite normal for her to be in and out of my house all the time. Or was – until you messed things up. And when you were staying with me the year before, we all saw that you were taken with Caroline –'

'She was only a child, barely out of school.'

'And she was more than a bit stuck on you. You are only ten years older than she, so don't go on as if you were her grandfather. It seemed a very suitable match to all of us.'

'To you and her mother, and, of course, dear Estelle, who just happened to arrive for a visit. How the three of you stayed friends all these years I have never understood. But that is beside the point. I'll choose my own wife, when the time comes.'

Josephine smiled, but without warmth.

'Well, well! Charles has made a good job of bringing you up. Quite in his own image. Heartless! You threw Caroline over because you want a woman who can advance your career. Poor kid!'

'Much you know about it!' Bernard retorted, stung. 'Why

didn't you ask Estelle? It may come as news to you, Mother, but she made very damn sure that that romance was never going to get off the ground.'

Marie-France was up in the little wood on the far slope of the valley. Looking across, she saw the two old men on the path on the other side of the lake, Grandpapa hobbling along on his stick, with the Colonel shortening his stride to match the slow pace. No need to wonder where they were going. Grandpapa was taking his daily walk to his precious grotto.

And that could be more than a little bit awkward. She had thought him safe in the house this afternoon.

Ahead of her lay a clearing, a private sort of place ringed with trees, and hidden from outside view. On a fallen log lounged a lean figure in jeans and an anorak.

'Chester!'

The tousled dark head turned in her direction.

'Hi!' he said, not getting up.

Marie-France's daydream of being crushed in a lover's warm embrace faded. That sort of thing was not Chester's style.

'You're late,' he said, as she approached. 'I'm halfway iced up.'

'I got away as soon as I could. The funeral was awful.'

'So I see,' he said, dispassionately. 'Your face is a mess. You've been crying.'

'It was *my mother*'s funeral.'

'You didn't seem to care all that much for her while she was alive. OK, kid, don't turn on the waterworks again. So you loved her all the time, underneath. Bully for you. As far as I could see, she didn't deserve it.'

'Chester, you are very hard.'

He shrugged. 'It's a tough world, honey.' His eyes wandered over her face, so much younger now in its grief. 'Believe me, you'll be better off without her. You'll be OK, once you have gotten rid of these relations and you've sorted through her things.'

Marie-France shuddered. 'I can't face that. Grandmama will have to do it.'

'Is that fair? She is a very old lady. However, suit yourself.'

'Now you are being beastly again. I suppose it is my job. But it's an awful thought.'

'I'll give you a hand if you like. But I warn you, I'll chuck most of it into the trash.'

Despite herself, Marie-France giggled.

'I'll have to smuggle you in. Imagine Grandpapa's face if you ran into him in the house! Will you really help?'

'Sure thing. Let me know when the coast is clear.'

Marie-France leant over to peck his cheek. The caress brought no response.

'I don't think I could endure this place without you. But, go now! Grandpapa is on his daily walk. He always comes up here when he's visited the grotto. I'll go and head him off.'

Chester stirred himself.

'See you tomorrow? Usual place? Or will the old man be prowling round?'

'He never goes out in the morning. Working on those silly old memoirs, on Grandmama's orders. Ten o'clock, then.'

Caroline wandered into the study. It was exactly as they had left it when Berthe came rushing in to tell them that the gardener had found Estelle in the lake. The General's notes were in neat piles on the desk, and her typewriter on the small table by the window was still uncovered, the sheet in it half-done. She sat down at it, wondering if it would be thought indecent to do a bit of work.

Bernard came in, heralding himself by a brief knock. He stopped short when he saw her.

'I'm sorry. I thought Uncle Léon might be here.'

'He isn't,' she said, unhelpfully, disconcerted to find herself alone with him.

'I can see that. What are you doing?'

'I thought I might as well get on with a bit of work.'

Bernard frowned. 'What work?'

'Don't you know? I'm typing Uncle Léon's memoirs.'

'Good God!'

'What's wrong with it?' Caroline snapped. 'I'm not totally useless, you know.'

'I never thought you were,' he replied, stiffly. 'I should

have thought you could have found something better to do.'

'Such as?'

'You seemed happy enough in the work you had last year. With an estate agent, wasn't it?'

'Fancy you remembering,' said Caroline, acidly, the memories all too clear-cut in her own mind. 'I wanted a change.'

'You can't build a career on changes whenever you feel like it.'

'Being a typist in an office isn't much of a career, either. Not in that estate agent's place, that is.'

'Does your mother approve?'

Caroline eyed him resentfully. Trust Bernard to put his finger straight onto the sore spot.

'I have no idea. I didn't ask her.'

Once again, a quick frown passed over his brow. 'I thought you two were good friends,' he said.

'We were,' Caroline acknowledged, annoyed at being driven into a corner, 'until she decided to present me with a step-father only five years older than myself. Younger than you, Bernard. She is forty and he is twenty-four. Can you imagine it?'

'You used to be all for Women's Lib.'

Caroline glared at him.

'That has nothing to do with it! Even you must see that I would not care to share a house with them.'

'You could have gone to your father.'

'No, thanks! I do my duty visits twice a year. Mother always insists, even though Daddy was the guilty party. *He* ran away from *us* to be with Marcia. I think she leads him a dog's life, too,' she added, a shade smugly.

'Your parents don't seem to choose second marriage partners very well,' Bernard observed drily.

Caroline suppressed a grin. She reminded herself sharply that Bernard must be kept at a very long arm's length.

'It's their own business, but that doesn't mean to say I have to put up with it.'

'I wondered why your mother didn't come for the funeral. She and Estelle were so close. Friends from schooldays.'

'She's in Australia with Alan, to meet his people. I don't know what they'll make of her,' Caroline added gloomily. 'They are stinking rich and he is the only child. I'll bet they thought he would bring home something better than my poor old mum.'

'She is a charming and attractive woman.'

'That was what Estelle was forever telling her. You know she spent most of her time either with us or with your mother. She was staying at our house when Alan appeared on the scene, but instead of dishing out advice, all she did was encourage her.' Caroline broke off, paused, then rushed on: 'It wasn't meant in kindness, Bernard. Estelle really enjoyed egging her on. It was as if she had been waiting for years to find some way of spoiling everything for us, and suddenly she had the opportunity.'

'Yet you let her bring you here, afterwards.'

'It was the only offer I had. And, if you must know, I thought I might find some way of paying her back. It's too late now, but don't ask me to be sorry she's drowned herself.'

'If she did,' said Bernard, coolly.

'An accident? Then it was Providence doing the rest of us a good turn.'

'If you'll take my advice, you'll keep your sentiments about Estelle to yourself. It wasn't an accident. Nor suicide. She was murdered.'

Chapter 2

From across the estuary, the cathedral carillon sang out the hour. Lottie checked her watch. Four o'clock. How could it be only four o'clock? The day had already gone on for ever.

She glanced round the familiar room, seeing it with new eyes: the windows with their painted shutters, the warm terracotta and ochre tiles on the floor, the dim ancient rugs, and the furniture that had outlasted several generations. Only the bed had changed. Her mother-in-law had had a great knobbly brass monstrosity, with a snow-white counterpane. Back in fashion now, she supposed, and wondered vaguely where it all was. Stuffed away in the attic, most likely. It would not have been thrown away. Sometimes it seemed to her that nothing had been thrown away here for hundreds of years.

Nothing but human lives.

Her thoughts dwelt on the bed, that chaste single cot lost against the length of the wall, which had stood there for thirty years. P.J., she thought: post-Josephine. A.J. there was a big *lit matrimonial*, now up in the attic alongside the brass, no doubt. Perhaps, if one poked hard and long enough in all the rambling outbuildings of the estate, one could find bits of the beds of every bride who had come to Keralic.

She switched off the light, and at once the room was swallowed up in the gloom of the louring sky outside, dark even for February. Bad weather was coming in from the sea and would be upon them by nightfall.

It was time to go downstairs, to find the unwelcome guests and pass on the message. They were all in ignorance, even Léon, for she had unplugged the telephone and carried it up to her room, for fear of missing something. The situation was

27

already too far out of hand to risk further confusion. So it was that she alone had received the call and had had time to adjust to the unpleasant necessity.

It would be interesting to see how much it upset them, she thought, descending the broad staircase that hugged the walls of the tower, down to the anteroom and the main entrance no one ever used.

She had hoped to find them all together, to deliver her bombshell. No such luck. The library was empty and littered with dirty coffee cups. (Where was Berthe?)

She opened one of the tall double doors that gave onto the drawing room. For a moment she thought that, too, was empty, then she spotted the top of a head over the back of an armchair. A smallish person, but not Marie-France, for the hair was chestnut. Josephine.

She would do, for starters. In a way, she was the best of the lot, since she must be the most uncomfortable guest in the house. Lottie was quite glad to have Josephine to herself. It came to her that the news would keep, since a much better opportunity was presenting itself: she had waited thirty years to stage a quarrel with Josephine, on ground of her own choosing.

'All alone?' she enquired, in a falsely friendly voice, advancing upon her quarry.

Josephine laid aside the magazine she had been leafing through idly.

'They have all scattered, Madame. I don't know where they are.'

Lottie sat down in a chair facing Josephine. What she saw frayed her temper. It was abominable that the woman should still have the figure of a girl, and not a streak of grey in the thick lovely hair. She had been forced to wear borrowed clothes for the unexpected funeral, and had looked wonderful in the dreariest rags to be found in the cupboards. Back in her own clothes now, she might have stepped straight out of the pages of that magazine on her lap.

Lottie took a deep breath to control herself. She could not destroy Josephine with screams of rage. 'They will appear by five,' she said. 'Looking for tea. Or had you forgotten that we keep the English custom here?'

She noted a quick flash of something – apprehension? – in Josephine's eyes, and was pleased.

'No, I hadn't forgotten.'

'I didn't think you would. What is it like, being back here for the first time in thirty years?'

And there it was, spoken: the question that had hung between them all the ten long days since Josephine's return to Keralic.

'And what do you think of my husband now?' Lottie swept on. 'Can you still see the man you knew in the dotard he has become?'

The colour drained out of Josephine's face, leaving rouge and lipstick spots of isolated pink.

'You are cruel.'

'I have every right.'

Lottie surveyed her victim, saw the desperate glance towards the door in the initial urge to flee, and the effort of will to force herself to remain and take what was coming, since there was no immediate way of escape. It was unfair that even so the slut was still beautiful, while she felt the blood coming up into her own face and knew that she must be turning an ugly brick-red.

'After thirty years, you are still bearing a grudge?' said Josephine, incredulously.

'Why not? You thought you could take my husband. First you took Estelle from me, and kept her, for she loved you ever after. And then you went after Léon.'

'I loved him, and he loved me in return. I don't know if he had ever loved you, but he certainly didn't at the time I came here.'

'He loved you?' said Lottie derisively. 'And what did it amount to, when the crunch came, and you found yourself pregnant? Your brave soldier turned out to be a louse.'

'I should be the one to call him that, not you,' said Josephine coldly. 'But I don't. My mistake was to believe that love conquers all. Dan Cupid didn't stand a chance against you.'

'*You* didn't, you mean. All you could offer him was a warm bed, and the children I was too old to bear. For a lot of men that would have been enough, but not for a Saint Brieuc.'

29

'Don't blame him. It was you who refused the divorce.'

'Of course. Marriage vows are made to be kept. But did you really think he meant it?'

Josephine stiffened. 'Why shouldn't he?'

Lottie showed her teeth in a thin smile. 'He couldn't afford the luxury. Keralic depends on me. The money was – and is – mine. The Saint Brieucs have nothing left. They have to marry cash. So Léon was caught by his own prudence. Ditch me and he could say goodbye to this place. I suppose you saw yourself as mistress here. Too bad! If I had let him go, you would have had to manage on his army pay in some scrubby little flat. And he would have hated you for it, because he loves Keralic more than anything in the world. No need to look so dumbstruck! You should thank me. I spared you that and I provided for you and the child.'

Josephine stared at her tormentor.

'Provided for me?'

'Certainly I did. Why do you suppose Charles de Montigny married you?' said Lottie, watching closely every fleeting change of expression. Suddenly, she crowed with laughter. 'Oh, don't tell me you thought Charles took you in out of *chivalry*? That really is rich. You were married to him for six years. Surely you must have discovered what he is.'

'Charles is a natural bachelor,' said Josephine, in a constricted tone.

'Selfish to the backbone. He was very hard up at the time. His old father was still alive and there never was such a skinflint. I can't imagine why Léon's mother married him, but widows often make disastrous second marriages, poor things. What sort of a father-in-law was he to you, Josephine?'

Her victim had had enough. She rose, elegantly.

'I don't wish to discuss Charles or his father with you, Madame. It isn't possible for me to leave here today, but I assure you I shall be going by the midday train tomorrow.'

Lottie grinned up at her.

'You won't, you know. There has been a message from the police. They're not satisfied that Estelle committed suicide after all. You have to stay here, every one of you, while they renew their investigations.'

* * *

30

There was a log fire burning in the big stone chimney of the study, bringing an atmosphere of instant comfort. Caroline had not put a match to it while Bernard was plaguing her with his wild ideas, but Colonel Clermont was a different matter. He seemed to be a nice old stick and he looked blue with cold. She closed the shutters against the advancing gloom, switched on the table lamps and the light in the niche containing a small stone statue. The flames sent shadows dancing on the heavy beams of the lofty ceiling.

They drew up easy chairs to the blaze.

'Where is the General?' Caroline asked.

Colonel Clermont jerked his head towards the door. 'Lying down. He wanted to take me all the way to the grotto, but he was making very heavy weather of it. I was just wondering how to tell him that I didn't think he could get there when Marie-France appeared and persuaded him to go back to the house. He was completely out of breath when we came in. Today has been too much for him. Perhaps he'll stay in bed.'

'It would be no trouble to bring him his dinner on a tray. I could do it, since I suppose Berthe would kick up a fuss.'

The General's rooms were on the ground floor, a suite of bedroom, bathroom and study, situated on the far side of the anteroom. Well away from Lottie, though all she had to do was open a door that was habitually shut. Yet she had never done so once since Caroline had been at Keralic. It was as if that part of the house was nothing to do with her.

'Am I interrupting your work, Mademoiselle?'

Caroline shook her head. 'No, I wasn't working. Just fiddling about. I didn't want to be in with the others.'

Colonel Clermont smiled.

'Now, there I am with you. Madame is not as I remembered her.'

'She certainly isn't. I haven't been here since I was about twelve. My father is her nephew, you know. We used to come here every year for a holiday, but my parents got divorced and Mummy wouldn't come again. I suppose she didn't like Aunt Lottie, or perhaps she felt it might be awkward. Yet she and Estelle were always such close friends. They were at school together – that's how Mummy met Daddy, through Estelle – and always kept up.'

31

'Did you like Estelle?'

Caroline pulled a face.

'Oh, she was all right, until a year or two ago. She was always having crises and would ring up Mummy from some far end of the world, to weep on her shoulder, and usually take the next plane for England. Nothing ever worked for her, you know. Her marriage collapsed, and after that she always had some terrible man in tow, someone quite impossible, and a few months later she would be on our doorstep, shattered.'

Colonel Clermont sighed.

'She was such a beautiful child,' he said. 'Seeing her for the first time for years last week was a terrible shock. She looked a wreck. Yet she can't have been much above forty.'

'That's right. My mother is forty, too,' Caroline agreed, thinking dark thoughts about the newly wedded pair in Australia. God! What a ludicrous mess!

'What happened to Estelle? The world should have been her oyster. She had everything. Looks, money, a good family,' said the old man. 'At one time, I hoped she and my son would make a match of it.'

Caroline smiled. 'I'm sure he would have been an improvement on the man she did marry. She had rotten taste in men, judging by the types she took up with in recent years. It's my belief that Estelle had too much. Aunt Lottie is frightfully rich, thanks to some old aunt who left her a bundle all to herself because my grandfather had blotted his copybook. Our branch of the family gets by, but we just aren't in the same league. Daddy used to go on about it.'

'So you don't want a lot of money?' asked the Colonel, amused. 'I thought all young women had endless need of funds.'

'Oh, I could spend it. I admit I have expensive tastes. But I wouldn't like to be married for my money. Estelle was.'

'I suppose so. He was a wastrel, sure enough. I hope Marie-France has not inherited anything from him.'

'More likely going her mother's way,' said Caroline. 'She is stuck on a grotty yob who lives on a boat in the port.'

'So I had gathered,' said the Colonel drily.

32

Caroline grinned. 'Anyone staying in this house for more than twenty-four hours would have to be blind and deaf not to know about Chester,' she said.

'Have you met him?'

'Once or twice.'

'What is he like?'

'There is more to him than meets the eye,' said Caroline. 'For a start, he's older than he pretends to be. Marie-France says he's twenty-two, but I reckon you could give him another ten years.'

'But what is the point of such a deception?'

Caroline shrugged. 'Search me! Perhaps he's afraid she'll think he has one foot in the grave if he owns up, since she's only eighteen.'

'Have you told her that?'

She laughed. 'Try telling Marie-France anything about her precious Chester! That one has to find out for herself. I don't want to get involved in that argument. No thanks!'

'Perhaps you are wise.'

'I have a strong sense of self-preservation,' said Caroline, flippantly, then sobered. 'There is one thing, though. Estelle was on drugs. Aunt Lottie won't even admit it, but I'm sure she was. I can't help thinking that the stuff is supposed to come in on little boats in quiet places.'

Léon lay on his bed just long enough to make sure that the Colonel had gone away. Then, very quietly, he emerged from his room. The muffled sound of voices from his study reassured him. Edouard and Caroline were in there.

One of the watchdogs safely out of the way.

He might be doing his old friend an injustice, but it was just a little bit too convenient that he had arrived hard on Josephine's heels. To appear so suddenly, and after so many years of silence, just when Lottie might be needing him most – ah! it was all too pat. He had never even seen the letter Edouard was supposed to have sent, asking if he might visit them. Lottie had told him about it, since, very correctly, it was addressed to her. It had to be a figment of Lottie's fertile imagination, to cover the summons of the old friend to help combat the unexpected menace. She was trying to cover it by her offhand manner to their guest, but Léon was not deceived.

Lottie was devious. He had been warned, the night before the wedding, by her own brother, black sheep George Bracebridge – young Caroline's grandfather – to cut and run before it was too late.

Did anyone ever take good advice?

Between his friend and his wife, he had not succeeded in having a word alone with Josephine.

And he owed her that much.

There was an outside chance that he might snatch a few minutes with her now, while Lottie still thought he was under Edouard's surveillance.

He crept down the corridor and across the anteroom.

It was a disappointment to find the library empty, still more so the drawing room. Josephine must be up in her room, and there he dared not go, even if he knew which one was hers. He went on, through the dining room and stopped short.

The kitchen door was open and there she was, a pair of rubber boots in her hand.

She did not look particularly pleased to see him.

'Josephine,' he said humbly, 'I was hoping to find you alone.'

Behind her, a clatter from the kitchen betrayed the presence of Berthe. Josephine put down the boots and shut the door.

'Well?' she said.

The words he had prepared died on his lips. 'What are you doing with those boots?' he said.

'I'm going to pack them.'

Léon nodded. 'I can understand that you don't wish to stay on here.'

'I should not have come in the first place,' said Josephine bleakly.

'I'm glad that you did. You have never been far from my thoughts, and I have prayed that I might see you once again before I died.'

She frowned.

'Please don't give me that, Léon. I know I was only a

34

passing fancy. You would never have given up Keralic for me.'

He stared.

'I don't understand.'

'No? Don't let's pretend. If you had obtained a divorce, you would have lost this place.'

Comprehension swept into the General's face. 'You've been talking to Lottie.'

'Yes, and she told me things that should have been made clear to me thirty years ago. The bargains that were made over my future, without consulting me at all.'

'There were bargains,' he admitted. 'Not only for you, but for Bernard, too. I tried to do my best for you, once it was clear that Lottie would not divorce me. I couldn't ask you to remain my mistress and let the child be born illegitimate. Not with what Lottie was offering you.'

'Offering?'

Léon sighed. 'I see that Lottie has told you only part of the story. I agreed to stay with her in return for a respectable marriage for you, and the right to watch over our child.'

The hostility died out of Josephine's face.

'Why didn't you tell me?'

'That was one of the conditions of the bargain. And I was afraid that you would refuse the offer. I was overwhelmed with guilt for my own weakness. You were only nineteen. I was over fifty. I had no right to have touched you.'

Two big tears welled up in Josephine's eyes. She snatched up the boots.

'You great silly!' she said, and ran out of the room.

Léon sat down at the table. He had not said any of the things he had intended, and he might not have another opportunity. Not if Lottie and Edouard had anything to do with it.

Presently, he rose and went into the kitchen. Berthe was washing the floor, muttering to herself. She turned up the volume for his benefit.

'I don't know why none of them stops to wipe their boots. Mud all over the place. And somebody has to clear it up.'

'I'm sorry you've been troubled, Berthe. We are very thoughtless.'

35

She sniffed. 'It's not to be wondered at, today, I suppose. And there is worse to come, General, you mark my words.'

He stared at her.

'How can there be?'

'She didn't do it.'

His head full of Josephine, he did not comprehend.

'What?'

'Drown herself.'

He shook his head. 'You mean she just blundered into the lake because she was too drunk to see where she was going?'

Berthe wrung out the floorcloth, viciously.

'Pushed!'

'Pushed?'

'You heard me, General. No one knows better than I that she was always threatening to do herself in, but she never meant it, not after that once, when she frightened herself as well as us.'

'How do you know? What she had done once, she could do again.'

Berthe snorted. 'Childish blackmail to get her own way, because she had never grown up. And it worked, didn't it, because you and Madame were always fighting over her like two dogs with one bone. So you danced to her tune. And that day was no different, was it?'

Léon reached for a chair and sat down heavily.

'No,' he agreed, wearily. 'I had given in. As usual.'

'Well, then!'

'But I had told her to get her mother's permission, too. And do you know what that was? Cowardice! Expecting Madame to pull my chestnuts out of the fire. I thought I could count on her to put her foot down over bringing that fellow here.'

'Ha!' Berthe exclaimed. 'So that was what it was all about. Fine fool she was making of herself. I don't know what is the matter with them these days. Not an idea of what is due to their family, though it's hardly fair to blame Marie-France when her mother set her such an example.'

'I was sure Madame would not receive Georges Quennec. Estelle insisted that she was going to marry him and have him here to live. The son of our butcher, Berthe! Perfectly respectable people, of course, but not suitable. I could not

36

bear the thought of Keralic falling into the hands of tradesmen.'

The old servant directed a sharp look at him, and a strange smile appeared on her face. 'Nor could someone else.'

The General stared at her, shaking his head slowly from side to side.

'Are you suggesting that she was *killed* because of that nonsense?'

'I'm trying to tell you what is going to be said, General,' Berthe replied grimly. 'All right, so she and Madame were screaming at each other before dinner. What of it? Estelle knew she would get her way in the end, because she always did. She'd beaten you, hadn't she?'

Léon clenched his hands so that the knuckles showed white.

'Berthe! Stop! Do you know what you are saying? If Estelle was pushed into the lake, it must be one of us who did it.'

Marie-France burst into the study, made for the fire and shook herself like a dog with a wet coat.

'Brrr! This is the only cheerful room in the place! Have you seen Grandmama?'

Caroline and the Colonel looked at her in some surprise. Marie-France had to be scraping the bottom of the barrel to seek their company.

'No,' said Caroline. 'Were you looking for her?'

Marie-France sat down on the rug and tucked up her feet beneath her.

'Goodness, no! I know where she is – in the kitchen with Grandpapa and Berthe. I thought she might have been in here to spread the glad news.'

'What news?' asked Caroline, warily, mistrusting the girl.

'That the police don't think *Maman* drowned herself.'

Marie-France looked round for the effect of her bombshell. The Colonel's face must have satisfied her.

'You've been talking to Bernard,' Caroline explained. 'Don't tell me Aunt Lottie believes any of that rubbish.'

'I can't imagine what Bernard has to do with it,' Marie-France replied, sulky and baffled. 'Grandmama had a phone call. We are all going to be grilled in the morning.'

'Grilled!' repeated the Colonel, astounded.

'And I know exactly what is going to happen,' Marie-France rushed on. 'You are all going to close ranks against Chester. Just because he is the outsider.'

'Rot!' said Caroline. 'Can't you ever think of anything except that wretched man?'

'You don't know what it is like to be in love! You are like Grandmama, cold-hearted. But I won't have him blamed, just because *Maman* was so beastly about him.'

'Your mother,' said Caroline caustically, 'was beastly to just about everybody. She must have made strings of enemies. If – and personally I don't believe a word of it – someone killed her, the police are going to have a field-day. There will be a queue of suspects from here to New York.'

Marie-France, fit to explode, drew a deep breath.

'I'm sure you've got it wrong, Marie-France,' the Colonel interposed before she could let off a broadside at Caroline. The mild tone seemed to calm her. 'If the police continue their enquiries, the result must be in favour of accidental death. The brutal fact is that your mother was drunk that night. That was painfully clear to us all after dinner, and would have been to you, too, had you been there. I trust the police will finish their investigations very quickly and let us go home. These days that I have spent here have been the most painful of my whole life. The last time I was here was for your mother's wedding, and I have seen none of the family since. To find you all as you are now has been a great shock to me.'

Marie-France jumped to her feet. 'You make my heart bleed!' she said rudely, and ran out of the room, slamming the door behind her.

The big stone chimney took exception to this and belched out a huge cloud of smoke.

Odile Quennec moved uncomfortably round her son's studio. It was another world, for all that it lay just down the hill from her own house. Of course, she knew that there were artists here and there along the coast, where once there were only fishermen, and the shops sold Breton carvings and pots to the tourists, but this was different. For one thing, it was Tremerrec, and for another, it was her own son. And she could not see any tourist buying his immense sculptures. Or anyone else. He scraped a living by doing part-time teaching.

Yet he was just back from that exhibition ... and he had won a prize.

She was proud but there was so much that she did not understand.

The studio was a big untidy room, the major part of a box-like building with a steep roof, almost as old as the town itself, right down on the quay, only yards from the boats for which it used to store cables and sails. The rest of the space was taken up by a small bedroom, bathroom and kitchen – a bachelor establishment, she thought suddenly.

'Were you going to bring Estelle here?' she asked.

Georges was tinkering with a large complex structure in thin shining strips of aluminium. Absorbed, he heard the voice but not the words.

'What was that?'

'Estelle. Was she willing to live here?'

'Hardly. If you must know, Mother, Estelle was as fully aware as you that neither Tremerrec nor Keralic would do for us, once we were married.'

'She had that much sense! What were you going to do?'

'Leave here. Both of us.'

'I suppose with her sort of money you can do that,' Odile observed, with a trace of envy. Not that she would ever have considered leaving Tremerrec, but it would have been nice to have the option.

'As a matter of fact, she was broke.'

'Never!'

'She was. You know there had been other men. Young ones mostly. On the take. She had been milked dry.'

Odile stiffened.

'How can you be so calm about them, those – lovers?'

'I had no illusions about Estelle, Mother. I know what sort of a life she had led. She was quite open about it.'

'Brazen!' Odile gasped, forgetting all her good resolutions about not speaking ill of the dead.

Georges shook his head. 'No. Just honest. For perhaps the first time in her life.'

'Honest!'

'With me. Not, perhaps, with other people. I am afraid she

39

tormented her mother with plans for bringing me to Keralic. The idea was to buy us off.'

Odile blinked. Was this really the little boy she had raised so carefully to know the difference between right and wrong?

'But that is immoral,' she protested. 'Georges, you should not have asked her to marry you when you couldn't support her.'

He laughed. 'Bourgeois values, Mother. There was no way I could ever have supported Estelle. What did it matter, anyway? The money would be hers eventually. She had her eye on a place in Provence for us. Good area that, for someone like me. Plenty of rich people who buy works of art.' He glanced at his latest creation. 'I am not going to sell that in Tremerrec, Mother.'

She looked at it, doubtfully. 'Georges, what is it?'

'Does it have to be anything? Ah, Mother, you haven't a clue, have you?'

'And Estelle had, I imagine?' she replied, slightly nettled.

He shook his head. 'No more than you, my dear.'

'I can't see why you had to choose her. There are lots of lovely girls in Tremerrec.'

'Who all want neat little houses with neat little gardens and neat little husbands with neat little jobs. I left all that behind when I went to art school. Oh, no, Mother, at least Estelle would not have enslaved me.'

'Don't you believe it! Oh, I'm sorry, I shouldn't have said that. She's dead and perhaps you would have been happy. I suppose it's no use telling you that you have to put it all behind you.'

Georges's face hardened. 'I can't put it behind me, Mother. Estelle didn't take her own life. She had too much to live for.'

'But those threats –'

'Childish nonsense. She tried that trick on me a few times, until she found it wouldn't work. I just laughed at her, as her parents should have done, years ago. No, Mother, she didn't commit suicide, and I don't believe it was an accident, either. She wasn't the type to go wandering about the garden at night in winter. They killed her, that lot.'

'Georges, that's just wild talk.'

'You'd better believe it!'

'But why should they?'

40

'Because she didn't fit in any more. Because she had become a liability. And they think they have bamboozled the police and the whole town. Maybe they have. But not me. And I'm going to make sure they pay for it.'

Josephine was packing her suitcase. Each item went in neatly folded because she was that sort of person, but accompanied by a running commentary on the manifold defects in Lottie de Saint Brieuc's character. She slammed down the lid with a final imprecation.

She could not help but remember the last time she had packed her things in this house. In this very room, next to Estelle's, overlooking the grassy courtyard in front of the house. Her eyes strayed to the connecting door between the rooms, and memory brought the ten-year-old child rushing through, tears streaming down her cheeks, demanding a promise of eternal friendship.

That was one promise she had kept.

Perhaps she should have broken it, severed the connections for ever. But there was always Bernard, to tie her, no matter how reluctantly, to the Saint Brieuc family. Nowadays, she thought suddenly, it would be all arranged differently: a quick abortion and that would be that.

There was a knock at the door. Josephine froze. If it were Lottie there would be no escape, short of climbing out of the window and a perilous descent of the wisteria. She did not fancy it.

The knock was repeated.

'Who is it?' she called, wondering why she bothered. Whoever was on the other side of the door was determined to come in.

'Bernard.'

It was on the tip of her tongue to tell him to go away, on the off-chance that he might obey. Then she recalled that he might be of service to her.

'Come in.'

And there he was, her only child, who could have been robbed of life before it ever started. What did she feel about him, apart from guilt – guilt of conception, guilt of abandonment?

More to the point, what did he feel about her?

41

He stood in the middle of the room, frowning at her suitcase.

'What's the idea, Mother?'

'I'm leaving.'

'Didn't Lottie tell you? You can't.'

'Correction, Bernard. All I am obliged to do is to be available for police questioning. I am not required to be a prisoner in this house. I'm moving into the hotel in the town.'

'You can't do that.'

Josephine snapped the locks of the case, then lifted it to the floor. 'Why not?' she retorted.

'People will talk.'

'Oh, for heaven's sake, Bernard! The whole of Brittany will be yapping its head off in a week if it turns out that Estelle was murdered.'

'Granted. All the more reason for us to stick together.'

Josephine eyed him coldly. 'But I am not one of your "us". I don't think I owe the Saint Brieucs anything. Least of all, Lottie.'

'You've been quarrelling.'

'It was not of my making. You don't imagine that I have enjoyed being back here, do you? And now my position here is totally intolerable. I should never have let Estelle persuade me into coming.'

'Why did you?' Bernard demanded.

'I was sorry for her.'

He let out a crack of laughter. 'Sorry for Estelle? Come on, Mother, that's a bit much even for you.'

Josephine shot him a look of acute dislike. 'It may come as a surprise to you, Bernard,' she said, 'but you don't know everything. Estelle was a pathetic, unhappy person, right from childhood.'

'What? She had everything.'

'Materially, yes. Children have other needs.'

'Like a mother, for instance.'

Josephine winced, and the hostility died out of her face. 'I suppose I deserved that, Bernard. Is it any good to say that I didn't want to leave you behind?'

'It is not natural for a mother to desert her child,' he replied, with a stony face.

42

She took a deep breath and faced her son. 'As I said, you don't know everything. Perhaps it is time that you did. It seems to me that I am the only person in this whole affair who has actually kept her word. It was supposed to be a secret for ever. Yet Estelle knew, and she told Marie-France, who has been giving me the benefit of her contempt since I set foot in Keralic. She told Olivia and Caroline, too, for that matter.'

'Told them what?'

She could not meet his eyes. 'The whole sordid tale of my youthful peccadillo. My attempt to snatch another woman's husband. And my failure. Every last miserable detail.'

'I thought she was supposed to be your friend. How long ago was this?'

'Four or five years ago. Before you started visiting me. I didn't hold it against Estelle. At the time, I don't think I cared. I was settled in England, and I never expected to see any of the French family again, not even you. I was sure Charles would prevent you, even if you wanted to see me.'

'He did his best,' said Bernard, grimly; 'but I am not easily put off. So, if everyone else knows, haven't I the right to know, too? Uncle Léon is my father?'

'Yes.'

'There is no doubt?'

She shook her head. 'The marriage I was pushed into was a marriage in name only. It was a cold-blooded bargain, and I accepted it because I daren't go home and admit what I had done. One-parent families weren't looked on with any favour in those days, let me tell you. So Lottie salvaged her pride, her husband and her home. Léon saw that our child was provided with a name and a suitable background. Charles was paid a lot of money to become your "father".'

'And you were to have a name, too, and respectability and an easy life. So why did you leave when I was six?'

'Because that was when Charles decided you could do without me.'

Bernard stared. 'He sent you away?'

'Yes. No one else knows that, and I'll thank you not to tell them. Charles never really accepted me. I wasn't good enough for him. He married me to please Léon. He thought the world of his brother.'

43

'Don't forget the money,' said Bernard, with an edge to his voice.

'Certainly he needed it, at the time, but truly I think it was mainly to do something for his brother's child. And he has done his duty by you, Bernard.'

He took a turn round the room.

'Mother, you are a very strange person. I don't know how you can be so calm about all this. You appear to be able to forgive Estelle everything. Does that extend to him – my "father"? I have to go on calling him that: what else can I do?'

Josephine thought for a moment. 'If acceptance of motive is forgiveness, I suppose it does. Charles has a great pride of family and descent. To save you for his brother, he was obliged to take on me. And it wasn't quite as bad as it sounds. He gave me enough money to buy a house and have an income.'

'And Estelle?' Bernard growled. 'Did you accept her motives, too?'

'If you are thinking about what happened last year with you and Caroline, I can't say. Until you told me, I didn't know that Estelle had involved herself in that quarrel. It seems pretty pointless to me. I imagine she was just trying to hit out at somebody. Her affair with that awful young man had just broken up and he had gone off with most of her money. She was in a very nervy state.'

'She was a bitch!'

Josephine sighed. 'She never stopped to think. When she was hurt, she wanted to hurt someone else in turn. Like a child. Yet all she wanted was to be loved.'

'She went about it in a mighty peculiar fashion.'

'You never knew her as I did. When I came here she clung to me from the first moment. Lottie worshipped her, but she didn't know how to manage children and she was too old to learn how. She became very jealous of me when she saw how Estelle took to me. I wasn't supposed to see Estelle after I was married, but I did. She was sent away to school and I used to visit her. Every time, she cried when I left. Eventually, she came to live with me, when I was back in England.'

'Lottie permitted that?'

'She didn't know. She thought Estelle was sharing a flat with her friend Olivia – Caroline's mother. It was a half-truth.

They were both with me. The three of us have stayed friends through marriages, divorces, disasters – whatever. And when I decided to leave London, naturally I went to live near Olivia. That has been the pattern of our lives for the past twenty years and more. Olivia and I always stood by Estelle. She needed us.'

'She used you.'

'What does that matter? Friends don't mind being used.'

Bernard stepped across to the window to close the shutters and draw the curtains.

'It's nearly dark. Mother, you can't go tonight.'

'I can, you know. Will you drive me into town, or do I have to call a taxi?'

'I think you should stay. It can't be for more than a day. The police may well have finished with you by the afternoon.'

She shrugged. 'So I only have to stay a couple of nights in Tremerrec.'

'Mother, please don't go.'

'Give me one good reason.'

'*I* am asking you.'

Josephine stared at him.

'I, too, have pride of family,' he said, with a rueful half-smile.

She sighed, knowing that she could not refuse him.

'Oh, very well, Bernard. But I shall expect you to leap to my defence if Lottie strikes again,' she added, with a forced lightness.

'I think you can ignore her pinpricks, Mother. The police, on the other hand, are a different matter. They are going to ask a lot of questions. Did they ask you many before?'

Josephine shook her head. 'Hardly any. Not with Léon so firm about suicide. I don't think I can tell them much.'

'They'll want to know what happened that night. In much greater detail.'

'I can't add to what I have already told them. We all had dinner at eight o'clock. It wasn't a particularly pleasant meal. We had all heard the row going on in the afternoon. Estelle got drunk.'

'Stop a minute,' said Bernard. 'What sort of drunk? Maudlin? Or happy?'

Josephine frowned. 'That's a good question,' she said at

last. 'I was so shocked by what happened afterwards that I stopped thinking about that evening. Over the years, I have seen Estelle in so many moods, and, yes, drunk as well as sober. She wasn't weepy and sorry for herself. In fact, I would say she was excited, keying herself up for something. That could fit the suicide theory, Bernard.'

'Perhaps,' he replied. 'The police will want to know where everyone was that night,'

'I doubt if we have an alibi between us. Marie-France rushed off straight after dinner. And the rest of us didn't hang around, once Estelle had made a little scene with Lottie. It looked like a continuation of the afternoon set-to, and I wanted no part in that. I went to bed.'

'And you stayed in your room till morning?'

Josephine hesitated. 'Now I come to think of it, I came down to get a book.'

'When?'

'I don't know. About half past ten, I should think.'

'And?'

'And nothing. There wasn't a soul about, although all the lights were still on. Bernard, that really is the lot. I don't know anything else.'

He eyed her for a moment. 'There is one question the police may not think to ask, unless someone tells them a bit of family history.'

'What is that?'

'Mother, what was it that Estelle brought you here to do?'

Chapter 3

Caroline discovered that Colonel Clermont was a practical
man. The chimney belched smoke, and an unwelcome rattle
heralded a fall of soot. The Colonel raced her to the brush
and shovel. Within minutes the window was open and
blowing cold but clean air, the soot cleared away and the fire
blazing brightly again. She blew a faint covering of black off
the top copy of the General's typescript.

'Is that the book?' asked the Colonel.

'Yes. As far as it goes.'

'And how far is that?'

'Oh, he's still at St Cyr as a cadet. Not much to show for
months of work, is it? I don't think Estelle was much help. She
was supposed to put his notes into order, but she found it
very dull.'

'And do you?'

She glanced across at him. He was long and lean and old in
a weathered sort of way – years of living in the sun, she
supposed – but his eyes were bright and he seemed
remarkably fit. Thick white hair covered his head.

'A bit,' she admitted. 'It should get more interesting later
on. I mean, he must have met so many famous people. You've
known him a long time?'

'We were at St Cyr together.'

She was surprised at that. 'Really? But the General—' She
broke off, in confusion. The words on the tip of her tongue
were hardly complimentary to her host.

Colonel Clermont smiled at her. It was a nice smile and the
teeth did not look to be false ones.

'I haven't got rheumatism,' he said gently. 'Léon is in a bad
way. I was shocked to see him. But I'm glad he's writing his

memoirs. The mind keeps going when the body stops, and it has to have something to do. I didn't know. Perhaps now I'm here I can give him a hand. I served under him in Indo-China. Are there notes about that?'

'I expect so. It will be months before we reach that campaign. I should think it was awful, wasn't it?'

For a moment, the Colonel did not reply.

'It brought out the best of Léon. Never have I respected him so much. But you are right. It was hell on wheels, as the Americans say. I sent in my papers after that, took the pension and settled in the south.' He glanced round the room. 'I think the smoke has cleared.'

'I'll shut the window,' said Caroline, anxious to show herself of some use. Something soft and cold blew in upon her. 'Goodness! It's snowing!'

'It won't be much,' said Lottie firmly. 'It hasn't snowed here for the past twenty years, until last month.'

Outside, the clouds ignored her. Snow fell steadily as the night closed in.

Berthe clapped the shutters into place as if she had a personal grievance against them. The curtains rattled along their rails, and the drawing room took on a veneer of good cheer.

From behind the tea-tray, Lottie glared at empty chairs. Everyone knew that tea was served promptly at five o'clock – a perpetual assertion of Englishness even after all these years – and the fact of a funeral in the morning would not alter the habit one jot.

'Where are they all?' she demanded.

The General started to struggle to his feet. 'I'll round them up.'

'You will do nothing of the sort,' said Lottie, venomously. 'If they are too lazy to come on time, they can do without.'

He subsided into his chair, and meekly accepted the cup that Berthe brought to him. The old servant waddled out, presumably to spread the news that tea was ready, regardless of her mistress's strictures.

Bernard came in, followed by his mother, her face like a mask. She sat down, speaking to no one, and allowed her son to act as cup-bearing go-between. Lottie shot milk into the tea as if she wished it were poison.

Berthe returned, shooing before her Marie-France, Caroline and the Colonel. Marie-France shook her head at a cup of tea, helped herself to a biscuit and went to perch on a radiator. The others sat down. For a while, only the rattle of cup on saucer broke an awkward silence.

Marie-France swung herself off the radiator, and lounged over to Bernard's chair.

'I hope you are satisfied, creep! The fuzz will be all over us in the morning.' She turned to the company at large. 'Did you know that we owe it all to stinking Bernard? Running about spreading stupid rumours. What he hopes to gain by it is beyond me.'

She paused for the effect and was rewarded. Lottie's face went slowly purple, while the General tried to struggle up. Josephine and Caroline both glared at Bernard. Only Berthe looked pleased.

'Traitor!' shrieked Lottie.

'Please, my dear, Lottie,' the Colonel interposed, on his feet and placing himself between her and her target, as if he anticipated a violent attack. 'This means nothing. There has been no question of foul play. If the new enquiry brings a different conclusion, it will be to establish accidental death, which has been my opinion all the time.'

Lottie turned on her husband. 'It's all your fault, you old fool. You insisted that Estelle committed suicide. And I know why, too. To get at me. Why else did you send her to me about the butcher's boy? As if I would ever receive him here!'

By this time, Bernard, too, was on his feet. He strolled over to the fireplace and stood with his back to it, surveying the company. He did not seem to be in the least perturbed by being everyone's idea of a pariah.

'I'm afraid you are wrong, Aunt,' he said calmly. 'As it happens, I said nothing to the police. I haven't spoken to any of them. The enquiry was already closed by the time I arrived, and I know only the facts which appeared in the report, which I was kindly permitted to read.'

'Oh, don't give us that, Bernard,' Caroline broke in, angrily. 'You *were* the one to start talking about murder, so don't pretend that you weren't.'

He ignored her. 'Myself, I have no evidence to present. I was not here at the time of Estelle's death. The pathologist found that she had died by drowning and the water in the lungs, as well as traces in other tissues, was the same as that of the lake.'

'Stop it!' Josephine cried. 'Do we have to go into these sickening details all over again?'

'She had a selection of bruises, including a big one on the side of the jaw,' Bernard went on, as if she had not spoken, and they listened in fascinated horror. 'There was also evidence on the path that she had fallen over. The level of alcohol in the blood was very high. And there was evidence that Estelle was in the habit of taking drugs.'

'That's it!' said the Colonel. 'A simple fall. First on the path and then into the lake. Tragic. Regrettable. But we really do have to get the thing into proportion.'

Bernard shook his head. 'I'm sorry, Colonel, but it won't do. I only wish it would. It's the common-sense view, and we must all hope and pray that the police findings will agree with you. But we can't count on it. It seems that there is evidence that has not been brought to light. In the initial enquiry, all the witnesses to what happened on the night she died came from this house. No outsiders.'

'How could there be outsiders?' demanded the General. 'We all know what happened. Estelle made a scene after dinner – all right, Edouard, I admit she was drunk, disgraceful though it was – and we all thought she had gone to bed. So we didn't go after her. We left her to sleep it off. It wasn't until the next morning that we discovered that she had not slept in her room, and about an hour later François found her in the lake.'

'No one heard her go out?'

'Bernard, what is the point of all this?' asked Josephine, agonised.

He glanced at her briefly. 'Believe it or not, I'm trying to help. I am not the one who has been stirring up the police.'

'Then, for heaven's sake who has?' demanded Lottie.

Bernard's eyes glimmered with an obscure enjoyment.

'You aren't going to like this, Aunt. It was your "butcher's boy", as you call him. Georges Quennec.'

Berthe laughed.

The bar on the quay was almost deserted, there being only one old man in a corner, when Chester Roach strolled in shortly before six o'clock. Behind the counter, Paul, the owner, was idly glancing through a newspaper. On seeing another customer, he brightened and, without asking, poured a Pastis.

'Thanks,' said Chester, adding water to the drink. 'Where is everyone?'

Paul shrugged. 'I expect they'll be in later. Unless the snow keeps them in,' he added, with an old sailor's contempt for the softness of landlubbers. 'How is it on that boat of yours? Cold, eh?'

'I keep warm enough. I thought you didn't have snow round here.'

'It's unusual. If it lasts till morning there'll be a fine old carry-on. They won't know what to do with it, and I doubt if there's a snow-plough anywhere in Brittany.' He paused, then added, slyly, 'It might stop your girlfriend from coming out tonight.'

Chester grinned. 'She's shut up with her ever-loving family. Tearing each other's eyes out, I shouldn't wonder.'

'It's a pity they have nothing better to do,' said Paul, with a temporary loss of memory over a certain split in his own family and with which he was passionately concerned. 'Had you heard? The police are reopening the enquiry.'

If he was hoping for an interested reaction, he was disappointed.

'Is that so?' said Chester, taking a gulp of his drink.

'And Georges Quennec is back, swearing she was killed.'

This time, there was a gleam in Chester's eye. 'They aren't going to like that,' he observed, laying a few coins on the counter to pay for the Pastis. 'I'll get back to the boat and batten down the hatches before it gets filled up with snow. Goodnight.'

Regretfully, Paul watched him go. The old man in the corner was stone deaf and in any case had gone to sleep. It was irritating not to be able to chew the fat – and what a piece

51

of fat! Estelle de Saint Brieuc had really landed her family in the mire this time. He was disappointed in Chester Roach. No natural curiosity. He reflected that the Americans were a strange race, and hippy ones the strangest of all. Nothing like Frenchmen.

He would have had more food for thought had he seen in which direction his departing customer walked. The boat lay a hundred yards downriver. Chester strode purposefully in the opposite direction.

There was no one about, and the snow fell steadily. The American squelched along, shoulders hunched, the dark cloth of his jacket glistening white. Ahead of him loomed the blank side of the old chandler's store. He turned alongside it towards a lighted window at the far end.

His knocks echoed, as if in an empty house, and no one hurried to open up. He persisted until at last the door swung wide. Georges Quennec, a black shape against the light, peered out.

'Oh, it's you. Come in.'

Chester stepped inside, shaking himself and stamping with his boots to get rid of the snow. Once inside and the door slammed against the weather, he looked at the older man, saw a grey and haggard face, smelt the brandy.

'I didn't know you were back.'

Georges passed a weary hand over his face. 'Late last night. Chester, why didn't they tell me? Someone could have. My parents – ah, but in their own way, they are as bad as the Saint Brieucs. Disapproval all round, old man. Come and have a drink.'

The studio, for all its size, was moderately warm, a closed stove burning in one corner. Chester accepted a share of the brandy, and settled down near the heat.

'Paul says the police are reopening the enquiry. Did you know?'

Georges let out a crack of bitter laughter. 'Know? I started that. This morning I was as mad as fire that I wasn't here sooner, so that I could say my piece, but on reflection I think it is better this way. Worse for them, that is. Just when they thought they had got away with murder!'

'What makes you think it was murder?' Chester enquired,

and added, hurriedly, at the look on his friend's face, 'Georges, I'm not doubting you. I would just like to know.'

Georges opened the stove and threw in another log. 'Estelle had everything to live for. She had it all worked out. I had a letter from her, in Tokyo. God! She must have been dead by the time I received it. All that suicide business was rubbish. There was a hell of a fight going on at Keralic. And Estelle was sure she was going to win.' He paused, and crossed to an untidy desk. From among a litter of papers, he fished out a letter. 'Here. Read for yourself.'

Chester unfolded the sheet covered with the late Estelle's untidy handwriting. He skipped through the opening paragraphs, then began reading carefully.

'. . . It really is going to work out. What a fool I was to let that ghastly Hugues run off with all my money – or what was left of it – you see, my darling, I really am trying to be totally open with you. I could kick myself when I think of all the wasted years when I didn't know you, and the way I have squandered everything Aunt Harriet left me. I never thought the day would come when I would be in need. However, all that is in the past. We are making a new start, even if I have to push a few people around in the process. My parents are sure to see sense. I have brought Josephine here, which is better than just threatening them with her from a distance, so Mother is certain to give way soon. After all, the money will come to me eventually, so I can't see why I should not be given an income now, when I need it. And in the long run, it should suit Mother better because we would hate to live with them as much as they would loathe to have the pair of us. I only keep on about bringing you to Keralic to make them nervy. Family pride and all that rot. I think we have the house, too. It should be arranged this week . . .'

'Well?' Georges demanded. 'Is that the letter of a suicide?'

Chester shook his head. 'No. I'll grant you that,' he said. 'But you know what they'll say. They'll insist on it being an accident.'

'Let them try! They'll have to explain why Estelle was wandering about the garden on a cold winter's night.'

'Everyone says she was drunk. Sorry to have to mention it.'

'Oh, I know all about that,' Georges acknowledged. 'She'd been on drugs, too. I had persuaded her to cut down on those and the drink. She wasn't the sort who could stand a complete break, and she didn't want to go for a cure until after we were married, in case the family shut her up in a nursing home and wouldn't let her out again. My guess is that they are all exaggerating about her state that night. She had promised me she wouldn't have more than a couple of drinks. But even if she forgot herself, Estelle would not have gone out, not without a good reason.'

'Fresh air?'

'Very fresh, in February! No, Chester, she went out to meet someone – to have the sort of talk they couldn't have in the house. She told me Berthe is always creeping around the place, keeping her ears open. But it would be a trap. Someone lured her out.'

'You're certain it was one of the family?'

'There's no one else around. She wouldn't ask an outsider to meet her by the lake. How would they find their way round the garden in the dark? It's not exactly small. Besides, who else had family pride and cash at stake? The only people in the world Estelle was threatening were her own.'

Caroline had retreated to the study. She was not surprised when first Josephine, then the Colonel and finally Marie-France crept in. She doubted if the others, locked in verbal combat in the drawing room, had even noticed their departure.

'What a performance!' Josephine exclaimed, pacing the room restlessly. 'How I wish I had not let Bernard persuade me to stay!'

'I thought you all had to,' said Marie-France.

'But not necessarily in this house,' Josephine replied crisply. 'I was proposing to go to the hotel. I am well aware that I am not welcome here.'

'More fool you for coming back,' Marie-France snapped. 'I

54

don't know why Grandmama let you over the doorstep.'

Caroline marched to the door, thrust it open and held it wide.

'One room in an uproar is quite enough,' she announced. 'We don't want any quarrelling here. There are three of us to one of you, Marie-France, so out you go or shut up.'

The younger girl glared at her for a moment, then her eyes fell.

'Have it your own way,' she muttered, and made no move.

Caroline took that as surrender. She shut the door and returned to the fire, upon which the Colonel, with utmost tact, was concentrating his attention.

Josephine wandered over to the window, pulled back the curtains, and opened one shutter. She cupped her hands to shade her eyes and peered out into the dark.

'It's still snowing,' she observed, closing the shutters and the curtains. 'Thanks, Caroline. You're a good girl, but I think I will go upstairs all the same.'

She drifted out of the room. 'Good riddance!' Marie-France called after her.

'You're a rotten little bitch,' said Caroline coldly.

Marie-France took it as a compliment. 'One has to be to survive in this house. I should have thought you would have discovered that by now. I don't know why *you* should defend Josephine. She made jolly sure you didn't get Bernard last year.'

Caroline was obliged to clench her fists to prevent herself from striking the other girl. She was surprised at herself. As if she cared a rush for Bernard de Montigny!

'I don't want to discuss Josephine with you, thank you! She is a close friend of my mother, and I have always found her a pleasant person.'

Marie-France sniffed.

'Suit yourself. The thought of her and Grandpapa together would make me sick if it weren't so funny.'

'I suppose you don't find yourself and Chester the least bit amusing?'

Colonel Clermont abandoned his contemplation of the flaming logs.

'Girls, please! All this bickering is a waste of time and energy. And in the face of an emergency!'

They stared at him.

'Yes, emergency,' he repeated, satisfied that he had caught their attention. 'Bernard does not strike me as a scaremonger, and indeed the fact that we shall all be questioned again tomorrow supports the position. This Georges Quennec must have some very special evidence to have persuaded the police to reopen the case. But why has he waited until now?'

'Oh, I can tell you that,' said Marie-France, not much interested. 'He was away at some exhibition. Tokyo, I think.'

Caroline stared. It did not sound a likely excursion for a butcher's boy. Or did the Japanese have special ways with meat?

'What sort of exhibition?' the Colonel asked.

Marie-France hunched a shoulder. 'Art, I suppose. Sculpture.'

'Art?' squeaked Caroline. 'I thought Georges was a butcher.'

'That's his father. The best meat in town, according to Berthe. Grandmama can't bear the thought that we still shop there, but Berthe insists. I expect she's related in some way. Tremerrec is very intermarried.'

'And what is Georges like?'

'Awful creep, if you want my candid opinion. He has a dingy studio on the quay. I shouldn't think he ever sells anything much.'

'But, my dear girl,' said the Colonel, in an astonished tone, 'If this Georges is exhibiting internationally, he must be an artist of both talent and repute.'

'I wouldn't know,' said Marie-France. 'He makes shapes out of old bits of metal. He hasn't any money and my mother had spent all hers, so unless Grandmama did something for them, they hadn't a chance. I'm surprised at you, Caroline, that you didn't catch on to what all those rows were about.'

'I only heard of him referred to as "the butcher's boy",' she said, aching to ask one question. It slipped out: 'How old is Georges?'

Marie-France grinned knowingly. 'Prize pair of mothers, ours! I don't know that it makes it any better that mine had given up cradle-snatching. She must have learnt her lesson with Hugues. Georges is mid-forties and already half-bald and grey. I suppose your mother's Alan is gorgeous?'

Caroline felt the blood rush up into her face.

'What I don't understand,' said Colonel Clermont hurriedly, 'is why Georges did not come straight back here as soon as he had the news of Estelle's death.'

'No one was bothering about Georges,' said Marie-France casually. 'You couldn't expect Grandmama to send for him.'

The Colonel muttered something about common courtesy. 'He must be a very angry man,' he added.

The library was an unexpected oasis of quiet. Thankfully Léon sank into an armchair. The nightmare had come upon them. He recognised it and acknowledged to himself that it had been at the back of his mind all the time. And, somehow, it was fitting that it should come through the agency of the despised Georges Quennec. The ruin of the house of Saint Brieuc was at hand.

If only he could talk to someone. . . .

As if in answer to his mute appeal, she came, walking softly through the door from the anteroom, wary of whom she might encounter. The light shone on her hair, turning it to a rich bronze and for a moment the old man saw her, once again, as she had been all those years ago.

'Josephine!'

She took the chair at the opposite side of the fireplace and they sat there, in false domesticity, divided by the lost years. She passed one hand over her face, the weary gesture destroying the illusion of youth, and he saw the mature woman who had grown out of the girl he had loved in one summer madness.

'You hate being here,' he said, and surprised himself.

What had he expected of her, catapulted back to Keralic after half a lifetime? How could he have been so wrapped up in himself as not to wonder?

'Yes,' she said quietly. 'This is no place for me.'

'Why did you let Estelle drag you here?'

She shrugged. 'Estelle had a way with her. I never did know how to refuse her. And, I must admit, it was a temptation.'

He drew in his breath. 'I don't flatter myself that it was to see me.'

'No. Though I did wonder what it would be like to see you again,' Josephine replied. 'It was something much baser. I saw a way of having a go at Lottie. You know what Estelle wanted me to do?'

He nodded. 'Lottie called it blackmail.'

'Quite right,' said Josephine, with a grim smile. 'That is exactly what it was.'

'You stood to gain nothing from it,' Léon pointed out.

'You're wrong there. If it had worked, I would have had my revenge on Lottie. I couldn't resist that. Thirty years ago she tried to arrange my life to a pattern she devised. I wasn't in any position to fight her—'

'My fault. I let you down.'

'So you did,' she said calmly. 'It took me a long time to come round to the view that I deserved it.'

'Josephine, don't! I have never forgiven myself for what I did to you. I should have given you the choice, but it seemed so much better to fall in with Lottie's plan. For you. And the child.'

'For you, too,' she reminded him. 'You saved Keralic.'

'Would you have defied the world and stayed with me, even with no hope of the divorce, if I had offered that?'

She sighed. 'At this distance of time, I don't know, Léon. Bernard would have suffered, and of the three of us, he is the innocent one. Would I have had the sense to see that Lottie's arrangement was, in fact, better?'

'You spoke of revenge a moment ago.'

'For refusing the divorce. That came as a terrible shock to me. Let's be honest about what happened. I took one look at you and decided that I wanted you. It never crossed my mind that I would fail. I made a dead set at you, Léon. It was a straight fight between Lottie and me, with no holds barred. I tried to take you from her. I was even stupid enough to think that getting pregnant would swing the balance to me.'

He put up a hand to cover his eyes. 'You make me feel like a piece of merchandise.'

'Oh, I loved you. I wasn't just on the grab. But I could see only my side of it. It never occurred to me that Lottie might *have* a side. I learnt, didn't I?'

58

'Were you very unhappy with Charles?'

'You know what he is. Not the marrying type. But he has always been very good to Bernard. He wouldn't let me take him with me when I went home,' she went on, carefully skirting the dangerous ground of the truth. 'He said Bernard must be brought up in France.'

'And you accepted that?'

It was her own fault for even mentioning Bernard. But it would do no good to reveal the hardness of Charles's heart. This poor old man had enough to bear without that.

'Bernard has never forgiven me for deserting him,' she said with a small sad smile. 'It is only in the last year or two that he has taken to visiting me. Why, I don't really know. I don't find him comfortable.'

'He's turned out very well. I'm proud of him.'

'Proud enough to acknowledge him as your son?'

Léon sighed. 'It's the thing I want most now that Estelle has gone. But I can't do it. I gave my word to Lottie. And I can't let the world laugh at Charles, either.'

'Estelle didn't share your delicacy,' Josephine pointed out. 'You know she wanted me to put a notice in all the Paris papers giving out the truth to the world – or whoever might chance to read it. And she insisted that I came back here to help her use that threat to screw money out of her mother. Not very nice, is it?'

'I can't blame you for wanting to get even with Lottie.'

Josephine shook her head. 'I blame myself for giving way to the temptation. It is all too petty, and it makes me feel soiled. I made a lot of mistakes and I hurt a lot of people, but I've learnt to make my own way.'

'It must have been very hard.'

Josephine smiled. 'The hard part was admitting to myself that I had made a shocking mess of my life. I bought a little house in London and took in Estelle and Olivia as lodgers when they left school. Then I went to classes to learn how to repair china. I found I could do it and started to work up a business. I've been doing it for twenty years now. I've no complaints.'

There was a short silence, then the General said slowly, 'Of the three of us, you have come out of it the best. Lottie and I – ah, well, I won't go into details, but we never succeeded in

59

rebuilding our family life. There was no way back for us. All we had was Estelle and we didn't even want to share her with each other. To her profit, of course. She played us off.'

'Poor Estelle. I suppose Lottie accuses me of being the bad influence?'

He sighed. 'It's easier that way, blaming someone else.'

'You really must stop torturing yourselves, both you and Lottie,' said Josephine sharply. 'Estelle was a grown woman and she lived the way she wanted to live. Her life had no direction. She never stuck at anything. When she and Olivia came to live with me in London they enrolled themselves in a secretarial school. Olivia worked at it, but Estelle was just playing. Then Henry Bracebridge swept Olivia off her feet in a whirlwind romance, and, without her friend, Estelle just dropped out. She had plenty of friends in London to idle about with, and no need to earn her own living. If anything destroyed Estelle it was that – too much money and nothing to do. Inevitably, she attracted undesirables. For what it's worth, I did my best to stop her marrying that impossible man. But she was infatuated. I might as well have been talking to a post.'

'Such a waste,' the General murmured. 'She was such a bright child. And we had such hopes for her. Josephine, is it possible, as Bernard insists, that she was murdered?'

Colonel Clermont decided that it ill-became a military man to skulk in his host's study for the simple reason that he was afraid of coming face to face with the lady of the house.

Lottie was a profoundly uncomfortable person to be with. Looking back, it seemed that she always was. It had been such a surprise when Léon, whom everyone thought to be a confirmed bachelor, had married that formidable English-woman. Neither a beauty nor in her first youth, either. But there was always the money.

He ventured out, down the corridor and into the ante-room, where, sure enough, Lottie pounced on him.

'Edouard! I've been looking for you.'

Colonel Clermont accepted his fate. There was no escaping from Lottie.

'Come and sit down,' she said, leading him over to the long

sofa against one wall. 'I need to talk to you.'

The big deserted room with the front door that was never used was hardly ideal for a cosy chat. On the other hand, there was no place for an eavesdropper to hide.

'I can't bear the thought of tomorrow,' said Lottie. 'The police back here, prying into everything, and all because of that butcher's boy's spite. That's what it is, Edouard. Pure spite. If only Estelle had listened to me, for once in her life. I told her, time and again, that he was no good. But did she take a blind bit of notice? Not she!'

'Children don't,' murmured the Colonel, searching unhappily for something to say. 'Michel never took any notice of me.'

'Ah, but that was different. You must be very proud of him.'

'I was disappointed when he would not join the Army. I thought he was mad, choosing politics. How wrong can you be? Look at him now, a member of the Government. My son a Minister! But it's a dangerous life, Lottie. At least a soldier knows who is the enemy. In politics there's always someone waiting to stab you in the back.'

'You're lucky, Edouard, to have such a son. My poor Estelle! I never understood how much she hated me until she came home this last time, bringing that woman with her.'

'Don't you think she was just desperate?'

'Desperate to humiliate me with the son of a local tradesman!' Lottie snapped.

'I gather he is an artist.'

She snorted her disgust. 'That cuts no ice here. In Tremerrec he is still the butcher's boy and Estelle was the heir of Keralic. Why couldn't she see that it was impossible? Edouard, I'm sorry. I didn't mean to go on about it. It's all done now and there is no help for us.'

'If there's anything I can do ...' offered the Colonel vaguely.

'There is. That's why I was looking for you.'

'If it's the matter of the grotto roof, I promised Léon to take a look at it, but I'm afraid I forgot all about it.'

'Oh, no, not that!' said Lottie scornfully. 'I don't know why he bothers so much about that wretched place. His father built it with his own hands, and not very well, either. That roof has given trouble for years, and it can fall in for all I care. No, Edouard, it's about Marie-France.'

The Colonel was startled. What did she imagine he could do for a young girl?

'I expect the police will let you go quickly,' Lottie swept on. 'There will be no need for you to stay on here, so as soon as you are free to go, will you please take Marie-France with you?'

He was taken aback.

'Well, of course . . . if you think . . .' he stuttered.

'Oh, please!' she said urgently. 'It's bad enough for the child that her mother is dead, and it doesn't matter that Estelle didn't pay much attention to her, she was still her mother. The police are going to pick Estelle's life to pieces. I want to spare Marie-France that. And I must get her away from that terrible Chester. Otherwise she is going to go the same way as her mother.'

'I don't know if I could make her very comfortable,' said the Colonel uneasily. 'I have lived alone since my wife died.'

'You have room enough, haven't you?'

'Oh, yes. The house is quite large. Most of the rooms are closed. She wouldn't find it much fun, shut up with an old man like me.'

'Better there than here,' said Lottie, grimly. 'You are my only hope, Edouard. I can't send her to England. Henry's second wife is impossible, and I can't see Charles helping out. We really are very short of relations, you know. The Saint Brieucs are nearly finished and the Bracebridges aren't much better.'

'Do you think Marie-France would go with me?' he asked doubtfully.

Lottie's lips set in an obstinate line.

'I'll see that she does! God alone knows what scandal is going to come out now.'

In the kitchen, Berthe was washing the cups and taking a long time over the job. There were things on her mind. It was all very well to take a peasant's pleasure in the discomfiture of her aristocratic employers, but the situation presented her with a problem. The police could prove tiresome.

Marie-France came in and flung herself into a chair by the table. She sat staring into space, idly chewing one fingernail.

'Going out?' Berthe enquired.

'It's snowing.'

'I doubt if it'll be much. It's not like you to mope about the house.'

Marie-France turned a sardonic eye on her. 'And it's not like you to care what I do.'

'I thought you might see Antoine in town,' said Berthe, trying to keep her voice casual. 'I might have a message for him.'

Marie-France was not deceived. 'I'll bet you have! What is it? "Run"?'

Berthe stiffened. 'Why shouldn't I send a message to my own nephew?'

The girl laughed. 'Especially when he has been in the habit of bringing my mother little unmarked packages.'

'How did you know that?' Berthe demanded, appalled.

'I keep my eyes open. She had to be getting the stuff from somewhere.'

'Antoine doesn't know what was in those packets. He was only earning a few francs. It's bad for a boy to be unemployed from the moment he leaves school.'

'I can hear the *flics* laughing at that one, Berthe. If you don't want to be mixed up in that lot yourself, you'd better ditch that no-good nephew. Sorry I can't help you out tonight. Grandmama has decreed that I have to stay in.'

'All right,' said Caroline firmly, 'let's have it. I'm sick of hints, and quarrels boiling up before anything has been explained so that in the end one knows nothing. Come on, Bernard, you started it. How come?'

Twenty-four hours ago, she would not have dreamed of seeking out Bernard de Montigny. Now she was glad to have him pinned down in the study.

'I told you. Georges Quennec.'

She felt irritated. He was sitting in the General's favourite chair, and, obscurely, that annoyed her, too. But most of all, it was his expression of calm superiority. She wished she could wipe it off his face.

'So you have a hotline to him.'

'Hardly. I didn't know who he was when he approached me in the cemetery.'

She stared, remembering the grim ceremony: the little family group, and the crowd of bystanders ranged round the boundary walls. And one man, bareheaded, standing in the no-man's-land between.

'He spoke to you? Why you?'

'I don't know. Suffice it that he did. I don't think he cared whom he told, as long as it was one of us.'

'What did he say?'

'That we had killed Estelle, but we need not imagine that we would be allowed to get away with it.'

'Is that all? Nothing else?'

'He mentioned a letter.'

'But, Bernard, the evidence? If it wasn't suicide, it has to have been an accident. And she really was legless that night. You weren't there. You didn't see her.'

'What was she doing out in the garden on a chilly February night? Don't tell me she had gone out for a breath of air. The lake is quite a way from the house,' Bernard reminded her. 'It was a peculiar thing to do, even for a tipsy lady. And Estelle wasn't one of the great outdoors type, was she?'

Caroline pulled a face, recalling incidents in times past.

'Goodness, no! She would hardly walk a yard if she could help it. She didn't care much for the garden, either. Bernard, what was in that letter? Or didn't he tell you?'

'Our conversation was necessarily brief. We were just about to come back to Keralic. But, yes, he did give me a hint – and I have no doubt that we shall hear all too much about it tomorrow from the police – that he believes Estelle went out that night to keep an appointment.'

'Oh, well, that surely lets all of us out. I mean, she could talk to any of us in the house. No need to go prancing round the garden in the dark.'

'It depends on what was to be said. How private a conversation can one have in this house? There always seems to be someone creeping about,' said Bernard dampeningly. 'I doubt if the police will make your assumption. Even if Georges Quennec would let them.'

'Whatever do you mean by that?' demanded Caroline crossly.

'Georges wasn't told that Estelle was dead. He was left to find out when he returned from Japan last night. Nor was he invited to attend the obsequies. He has taken it all very badly. Now he is yelling murder and he is hopping after the Saint Brieuc family and friends – all of us – with a well-sharpened hatchet.'

Chapter 4

The whole world was white. Snow lay thick everywhere, hiding grass and bushes, weighing down branches, peaking on the roofs of the twin pavilions of the lower courtyard. The big oak tree stood out, dark against the glistening mantle of the valley slope. It was as if all colour had been washed out of the universe, leaving only the stark alternatives of black and white, and a cold grey sky.

Berthe bustled into the dining room, bearing fresh coffee and news.

'François phoned,' she announced, with relish, to the room in general. 'The lane is blocked with drifts. He can't get through.'

If the gardener can't, then neither can the police, thought Caroline, and wondered why it seemed a relief when it could only be a postponement of the inevitable.

She observed that Berthe was looking pleased.

They were thin on the ground that morning. No sign of either Lottie or the General. Josephine never appeared for breakfast. The Colonel had taken on the task of operating the toaster. On the other side of the table, Marie-France and Bernard never uttered a word except to ask for the butter or jam. A morgue, Caroline reflected, might well be jollier.

'I suppose the police will have their hands full this morning,' said Bernard suddenly. 'We'll have to wait.'

He sounded disappointed. Caroline glowered at him.

'Who cares?' asked Marie-France.

'I do, for one,' said the Colonel. 'I'm all for getting it over. I want to go home.' He folded his napkin and marched out of the dining room.

A few moments later, Bernard followed him, leaving the two girls together.

'I'm sorry about yesterday,' said Marie-France, unexpectedly. 'I was a bore.'

'You were,' Caroline agreed, seeing no future in a polite disclaimer.

'I feel like a louse. *Maman* and I were forever having rows, and I was giving her hell over Georges. I thought she was ridiculous still looking for romance at her age.'

'You wait till you're forty.'

'I should hope I would be past it by then. What do you think about *your* mother? I've noticed you clam up the moment anyone mentions her.'

Caroline sighed. Clearly this was All-Girls-Together-Day.

'I'm with you,' she admitted. 'I think she is making a fool of herself. But the case isn't the same. Georges isn't young, like Alan.'

'My mother,' said Marie-France bitterly, 'did nothing but make a fool of herself. And got killed for it.'

'You believe in this murder theory?' cried Caroline, astonished.

'Yes, but poor old Georges has got it wrong. He thinks we – the family – fixed it somehow. That means Grandmama.'

Caroline had a vivid mental picture of Lottie pushing her daughter into the lake. Despite her advanced age, she was capable of doing it, given the element of surprise, and with Estelle fuddled with drink. She realised that she, too, had Lottie cast as First Murderer.

'But you don't think so? At least you have some loyalty to your grandmother.'

Marie-France shook her head. 'Don't count on it. If I thought she'd done it, I wouldn't lift a finger to help her. You can't imagine how sick I am of family pride and all that rot. No, Caroline, I don't know if the police will be able to uncover who was at the back of it, but my mother was mixed up with drug pedlars. They are not nice people.'

'You think they killed her?'

'It makes more sense than a pair of senile aristocrats, doesn't it? Particularly since Georges was trying to get *Maman* off the drugs. Once she'd stopped, she'd be a possible danger to her suppliers, wouldn't she?'

Caroline gazed at Marie-France with new respect. 'You have thought this out,' she said.

Marie-France pushed back her chair. 'I keep my eyes and my ears open. What's the time?'

'Half past nine.'

'Time to put my boots on. Chester doesn't like to be kept waiting.'

'The lane is blocked. He won't come.'

Marie-France laughed. 'He doesn't come up the lane. He rows the dinghy across to the bay.' She ran to the kitchen door, then paused and glanced back. 'I don't know what I would do without Chester. He's going to help me sort out *Maman*'s things. I shall have to smuggle him in!'

Caroline did not care for the sound of that. Chester would have an axe of his own to grind. Altruism did not ring true for him. So why should he want to get into Estelle's room?

She was filled with a sudden and inexplicable desire to discuss the question with Bernard.

The door to the drawing room opened, and she spun round in the hope that it might be he. Instead, Lottie stood there, her mouth set in a grim line.

'Ah, Caroline! I was looking for you.'

The girl's heart sank. She made a rapid scan of her conscience, looking for some fault.

Lottie raised her voice to call for breakfast and was answered by an eldritch screech from Berthe in the kitchen. Lottie took her place at the table.

'It isn't easy to get someone on their own in this house at the moment,' Lottie observed in a gentler tone. 'I'm glad I've found you.' She paused to look over her victim, and Caroline felt the blood come up into her face. 'I don't approve of you making eyes at Bernard,' she went on, chillingly.

Caroline stared at her aghast. 'Making eyes!'

She all but choked over the old-fashioned phrase.

'You may well blush, child! I've been watching you.'

'Then you've seen something that isn't there, Aunt. Bernard is nothing to me.'

'I'm not a fool. Or blind. What about last year?'

'Finished and done with, Aunt. Estelle opened my eyes for me.'

Lottie grunted. 'So she told me. Bernard was the one subject on which we saw eye to eye. But you beware of

Bernard or you will get hurt. He's ambitious and I can't see him marrying any girl who doesn't bring him some advantage.'

'There isn't any question of it,' said Caroline, ruffled.

'I'm glad to hear it,' said Lottie sourly, and in a disbelieving tone. 'Generally, girls are fools.'

Bernard himself was pacing the floor of his mother's bedroom. Propped up on pillows, Josephine regarded him with irritation.

'These matters are best left to the police,' she said firmly. 'The more we talk among ourselves, the more confused we are going to become.'

Her son came to a halt. 'That is remarkably good sense, Mother.'

'So what are you trying to do? Muddy the waters so that the police won't uncover the truth?'

'Not at all,' Bernard snapped. 'This thing could blow up into a big scandal.'

'Oh, I see. You want to hush it up. Fat chance if it does turn out that Estelle was murdered.'

'The police are going to dig into motives. Damn it, Mother, it's Caroline I'm worried about.'

'Caroline?'

'She made it quite clear to me that she doesn't think Estelle is much loss. How many other people has she told?'

'Don't be ridiculous!' said Josephine. 'No one is going to suspect Caroline.'

'I shouldn't count on that. I can't see the police buying Georges's theory about the old people, but once that's out of the way, there's not a great deal of choice of suspects in this house.'

'I must say you are a great comfort, Bernard!' Josephine remarked.

'Mother, is it true that Estelle encouraged Olivia to marry that young man?'

Josephine sighed. 'I'm afraid she did. I was surprised, after her dreadful experience with Hugues. I would have thought she might try to save her friend from a similar fate. Though the case is entirely different. Alan is not a fortune hunter. On the contrary, I fear that Olivia may be accused of that.'

'And Caroline was very upset?'

Josephine could not deny it. She nodded.

'Unreasonably so?' Bernard persisted.

'I thought so,' Josephine admitted. 'Since her parents split up she has tended to be possessive about her mother. There's no getting away from the fact that Alan has taken Olivia away from her. Caroline has refused to live with them.'

'And she blames Estelle?'

'She does. But you can't seriously suspect Caroline of *murder*?'

'I don't. But then I know her. The police don't. They could give her a rough time. I wish I could think of some way to protect her.'

Josephine eyed her son. 'That is just about the last sentiment I would expect to hear you voice,' she said drily.

'She can't be left to struggle on her own,' he replied curtly.

Odile Quennec picked her way slowly down the steep hill to the port. It was only rarely that she felt her sixty-seven years, but this morning each one weighed heavily upon her. And it was nothing to do with the snow, although the walking was worse than she ever remembered.

She found her son unoccupied, his tools idle. A pot of coffee sat on the top of the stove.

'Mother, what brings you here?' he asked, surprised. 'You must not make a habit of dropping in on me. Father wouldn't approve.'

The tone was light, but bitterness showed through.

She sat down near the stove, holding out her hands to the heat.

'We need to talk, Georges.'

'What about? Don't tell me you want to know about Estelle?'

'I do.'

'You would never listen to me when she was alive.'

'I expect that was wrong of me,' she said quietly.

Georges looked down at her in exasperation. Then he fetched a cup, poured coffee and handed it to her.

'I can't quarrel with you, Mother. You are caught between me and Father, and we both are stiff-necked. What do you want to know about Estelle?'

70

She took a sip of coffee. 'Was she on drugs?'

'Does it matter now?'

'I'm afraid that it does, Georges. I had a strange phone call from Berthe Guegan last night. She wanted me to take a message to her brother's boy, Antoine.'

'Why you?'

'Well, we are related. Aline hasn't paid her telephone bill and they've been cut off.'

'So you turned out in the snow? Good of you, Mother.'

She winced at his tone. 'You think I would help Antoine when I wouldn't do anything for you and Estelle? Believe me, I wanted to, but my first duty is to your father. Since that last heart attack, I'm afraid to upset him.'

'All right, Mother, you can cut out the violins,' he said roughly.

She stared at him, uncomprehending.

'Forget it,' he said. 'So Berthe is worried about Antoine. That boy is a spoilt brat.'

'What can you expect when a man marries so late in life and then dies when the children are young? Aline certainly has spoilt the boy, but that's beside the point now. Antoine could be in trouble. Berthe says he used to bring Estelle little packets.'

'My god! What did you do? Pass on the message? I suppose it was a warning about the police.'

'More. Marie-France has found out,' she said. 'I didn't know what to do. Drug-trafficking is evil. I went round there and told Aline she had better take Antoine straight to the Gendarmerie. If he leads them to the men who supply the stuff, they might let him off.'

'I can just see Aline doing that!' said Georges, with a crack of laughter. 'Don't you interfere, Mother. I hope Marie-France has not been shooting off her mouth to her family. That lot at Keralic will seize on this as a way out for them. I wouldn't like that.'

'I don't know why we never thought of it,' said Léon, in an astonished tone. 'The criminals who run the drug trade are totally ruthless. Yet it never crossed my mind.'

Caroline glanced round at the company assembled in the drawing room for the pre-luncheon *apéritif*: the General and his old comrade in deep armchairs, Bernard and herself at each end of the big curved sofa, Josephine in a low chair. Each face – and that must include her own – bore traces of relief.

'You were too busy beating your breasts,' said Josephine crisply. 'Admittedly, it is natural for parents to blame themselves for how their children turn out, but it's not logical. People have to make their own choices, and if they happen to be bad ones, that's just hard luck. Estelle wasn't obliged to take drugs. She did it because she fell in with a set of people who thought it was smart to smoke pot, and it went on from there.'

'She hid it from us,' murmured Léon.

'From me, too,' said Josephine. 'I found out two or three months ago. But it has been only in the last year or so. She wasn't too far gone. Not so that she could not be brought back. Give Georges the credit for trying.'

'He won't want it if that is why she was killed,' Caroline pointed out. 'Do drug-pushers polish off ex-customers?'

'It depends how much they know about the organisation that supplies them,' said Bernard. 'What else did Marie-France say?'

'Nothing specific, but I had the impression that she really does know something. Am I the only person she told?'

No one spoke up.

'It looks as though you are,' said Bernard.

Caroline thought she detected a note of disbelief in his voice.

'Ask Marie-France yourself!' she suggested, sharply.

'Don't worry, I will. Where is she, anyway?'

'Can't you guess? Gone off to meet her precious Chester.'

'In this weather?' the Colonel exclaimed.

'Love will find a way,' said Caroline airily. 'Actually, I thought Chester was the most likely person to be Estelle's supplier.'

'If only it could be proved that Estelle was killed because she knew too much about the filthy trade!' said Léon wistfully.

'It would be highly satisfactory,' said Bernard. 'But the police have to catch them for the suspicion to be removed from this house. As far as the rest of the world is concerned, that is!'

'When will the police be here?' asked Caroline, anxious now for them to come and get on with the job.

'When the Commune have got round to clearing the lane,' said Léon. 'I expect the police have their hands full, too, with traffic accidents. I doubt that they will come today.'

For the first time since his daughter's death, the old man sounded, if not quite cheerful, certainly lively.

In the adjoining library the phone began to ring. Bernard jumped up, but at that moment the sound stopped and vague echoes of Lottie's voice came through the door. Then she appeared.

'The police will be here very soon. The road is being cleared now,' she announced. 'The snow must have gone to their heads, if the sacred hour of *déjeuner* is to be waived. It isn't as though we are going to run away. If they want to starve, that's their business. We might as well have luncheon. It's nearly twelve.' She glanced round. 'Where is Marie-France?'

'Out,' Caroline informed her.

'Silly child,' said Lottie, mildly, and led the way into the dining room. 'I don't suppose it matters,' she said, over her shoulder. 'The police can't have much to say to her.'

Don't you believe it! thought Caroline. Trust Marie-France to be missing when wanted.

It was the first normal meal for days, with plenty to talk about. And, for once, everyone had stopped looking at each other out of the corners of their eyes. They had reached the fruit stage when a police car came slithering down the drive. With one accord, they left the table and crowded into the kitchen.

Five gendarmes jumped out of the car, opened up the boot and took out shovels, then briskly set about clearing snow from the courtyard. The family, assembled at the door, watched in amazement.

Then another car appeared, this time containing the highest-ranking officer that Tremerrec could boast. Behind that, another car, a van and an ambulance. The courtyard was jammed with vehicles.

The senior man, burly and impressive in his dark uniform, approached the house. Under his arm he carried a briefcase. Behind him came a young gendarme.

They came to a halt before the group at the kitchen door. All eyes fixed themselves on the big man. They knew him, of course. Brigadier Kergrist.

'If you would all be so good as to go inside ...' he said smoothly.

Like sheep, they backed away from him and returned to the dining room, and stood about, awkwardly, each aware that this large police presence was not what they had expected.

'That's an *ambulance*,' Caroline whispered.

'Shush!' said Bernard, as Kergrist followed them in.

The policeman singled out the General. 'I regret the necessity for this, Monsieur,' he said formally. 'I have to inform you that at shortly after ten-thirty this morning we received notification of a fatality here.'

'Nonsense!' said Léon. 'That's not possible. As you see, the snow is deep here, and until the lane was cleared we were cut off. My gardener could not get through. We are all present and—' He stopped, and there was an appalled silence. 'Oh, God!' he croaked. 'Not Marie-France?'

'I regret, Monsieur, yes.'

Lottie let out a piercing cry and there was instant hubbub in the room. The General's face turned an alarming colour. Between them, Josephine and the Colonel got him to a chair, while Bernard fetched a glass of water. Caroline found herself supporting the considerable weight of Lottie, who sagged unexpectedly against her great-niece.

'Ladies and gentlemen, I suggest that you all sit down,' said Kergrist, not without sympathy.

They ranged themselves round the table, still laden with the remains of their meal.

'What happened?' Bernard demanded, voicing all thoughts. 'How could anything have happened to Marie-France without us knowing. Are you sure she is dead?'

'Yes, Monsieur. I have seen the body. One of you will be required to make the official identification, but I have been in Tremerrec for twenty years. I have known her since she was a child,' he added, heavily. 'It is Marie-France.'

'Where? And how?'

'At the bottom of this garden there is a small building—'

'The grotto!' Léon gasped.

74

'Exactly. A grotto. The roof has collapsed. The young lady was inside.'

Lottie sat bolt upright. 'I knew it! How many times have I said there would be an accident? That thing has been unsafe for years.'

'Just a minute, Aunt,' Bernard interposed. 'Brigadier, you said you received notification. How could you? No one has been down there. Or have they?' he added, searching the group of shocked faces.

Mutely, they shook their heads.

'The information did not come from this house,' said Kergrist. 'It was from someone in a call-box.'

'Who?' Lottie exploded.

'We don't know, Madame. The caller would not give his name. He told us the girl was dead. I sent a car, but we found the lane was blocked by drifts, so I commandeered a boat—'

'That's it!' Caroline cut in. 'Chester. He must have been your caller. Marie-France was meeting him this morning, and it would be at the grotto, as usual, I imagine. He rows across in his dinghy.'

The Brigadier inclined his head.

'Thank you, Mademoiselle. That is very helpful. Tell me about this Chester.'

'American,' said Caroline promptly. 'Lives on a boat in the port. Doesn't seem to do any work. Tall, dark, scruffy. Says he is twenty-something, but I think he is older.'

'Admirable!' murmured Bernard, and earned himself a black look from both Caroline and Kergrist.

'Now tell me one thing more,' the Brigadier invited the company at large. 'How many of you, apart from Mademoiselle Bracebridge, knew that the young lady was in the habit of meeting this Chester at the grotto?'

There was a moment's silence.

Then Josephine said, 'I didn't.'

'Nor I,' muttered the Colonel.

'I have been here only a short time, as you know, Brigadier,' Josephine elaborated. 'And I was not in Marie-France's confidence.'

The Colonel shook his head. 'Oh, the poor child!' he said, in a shaken voice.

In the doorway, the young gendarme was making notes.

'Just a minute,' said Bernard, his voice sharp with suspicion. 'What does that matter?'

'A good deal, Monsieur,' Kergrist replied, grimly. 'The roof of the grotto did not collapse of its own accord, nor beneath the unaccustomed weight of the snow. A preliminary examination suggests that it had been rigged to give way a few minutes after the iron grille was opened – just enough time for the intended victim to walk into the middle. In other words, ladies and gentlemen, a lethal trap.'

Out in the kitchen, Berthe let out a piercing scream.

Caroline took one last look at the bed and decided that the sedative had done its work. Poor old Aunt Lottie, downed at last! Huddled under the blankets, she looked old and shrunken, nothing but the shell of a once-forceful woman.

She turned out the bedside lamp, closed the door quietly and went downstairs. In the library, she was glad to find Josephine, the Colonel and Bernard sitting round the fire. It was not the moment to be alone.

She sat down beside Josephine on the sofa.

'How is she?' asked the Colonel.

'Sleeping. I thought the stuff the doctor gave her was never going to work. But she's off now. How about Uncle Léon?'

'Also asleep,' said Josephine, to whom it had fallen to look after the General. 'For what good it will do. When the poor things wake up nothing will be changed.'

'And where is Berthe?' Caroline enquired. 'I had no idea she was so fond of Marie-France. I never expected her to go off the deep end like that. She was worse than Aunt Lottie.'

'She has barricaded herself in her room,' Bernard told her. 'Even the police haven't been able to get her to come out yet, but she can't put them off for ever. As soon as Kergrist has finished outside, he'll be here to take statements from all of us.'

'The police are still here?'

Bernard grinned. 'All over the garden. And they are here to stay. Some poor sods are going to have a cold night. The temperature is dropping like a stone. I know. I've been out.'

'What for?'

'I had to make the identification.'

76

Caroline shuddered. 'What is it like down there?'

'A mess,' Bernard admitted. 'I'm no expert, but with that load on top of her, it must have been pretty quick.'

'Is she still there?'

'Yes. They can't move her until the forensic team has done its stuff. And they are stuck in the snow somewhere between here and Lannion.'

'But that's awful!' Josephine exclaimed. 'They can't leave her there all night.'

'Mother, I know it sounds callous, but it doesn't make any difference to poor Marie-France where she is.'

'Bernard! You're disgusting!'

'Only a realist. But if it makes you feel any better, they'll move her as soon as they can.'

Josephine passed her hand over her eyes. 'I can't really believe all this. Is it possible to make a roof collapse like that?'

Bernard looked at the Colonel. 'What about it, sir? You used to be a demolition expert. What do you think?'

Colonel Clermont raised his head. His face had lost its usual colour. He, like the other old people in the house, looked frail and shaken. Caroline wondered if the hastily summoned family doctor should have taken a look at him, too.

'I worked with explosives. Bridges, mainly. But I do know a bit about structures. I am trying to visualise that roof. Léon asked me to take a look at it and tell him what should be done to make it safe. Then Estelle died, and I didn't give it another thought. Now I find I can't remember much about that roof.'

'It's a vault,' said Bernard. 'With a hole in the middle to let in light.'

The Colonel nodded. 'That's right. I remember now. And there is an iron gate to the place. Is that always kept shut?'

'Shut and locked,' said Caroline. 'Gangs of boys sometimes come over the river from Tremerrec. They did some damage there last month, so Uncle Léon decided to keep it locked. We hid the key under a loose stone at the side. Pretty obvious sort of place, I suppose. Why? Oh, that was what Brigadier Kergrist meant – whatever set off the trap was attached to the gate?'

'Bright girl!' Bernard murmured.

'As I understand him,' said the Colonel.

'Attached to the stones of the roof in some way so that one tug would pull it down,' Bernard added.

'Something of the sort,' said Colonel Clermont. 'Not over-difficult, if the vault is in as bad a state as Léon says. Bernard, you've been down there. What did you see?'

'Only a heap of stones. I wasn't given a chance to examine them.'

'I don't know how you can discuss it so calmly,' said Josephine, in a low voice. 'Who would set a trap like that for a young girl like Marie-France?'

Her words brought instant silence.

'You are right, of course,' said Caroline, breaking it at last. 'Marie-France could be a pill at times, but she wasn't a bad kid. Who on earth would want to *murder* her?'

The news sped round Tremerrec. It reached the butcher's shop in the shadow of the cathedral around three in the afternoon. By closing time, Odile Quennec had heard half a dozen different versions, some highly fanciful. But all shared a common fact. Marie-France had been murdered.

Odile was worried. Her first thought had been to rush round to the Gendarmerie, but she had held back.

She kept to her busy routine. Cash up the till and wipe the counters, while her husband cleaned the mincer. Then back upstairs to start preparations for dinner, which had to be early that night to enable her to be on time for choir practice.

Her problem refused to be driven away by sheer hard work.

At half past seven, she left her husband dozing in front of the television, and went out of the house fully intending to walk the few steps to the cathedral. Instead, she slithered over the snow, hard-packed now by many feet, down the hill to the quay.

She found her son reading and smoking peacefully beside his stove.

'What's the matter, Mother? It isn't Father, is it?'

She was pleased and touched by his concern. A sharp hope shot through her that, without Estelle to divide them, peace could be made between father and son.

78

'No, Georges, he's fine.' She took another look at him. 'Haven't you heard?'

'Heard what? I've been in all day. I thought the police might want a word with me.'

'They have other things to do. You must be the only person in Tremerrec who doesn't know. Estelle's daughter – Marie-France – has been murdered.'

Georges stared at her, unbelieving. 'Marie-France? It's not possible!'

'But it is! There is a tale of the roof of a grotto collapsing. I don't know if that's true. But whatever it was, the police have set up a murder enquiry. All afternoon I have been trying to decide what to do. Now I know that I can't just stand aside and pretend I am not involved. So I'm going to the police, Georges, to tell them about that message last night. I doubt if Aline has done anything about it.'

She rushed out, leaving him staring after her.

Brigadier Kergrist appeared at the kitchen door after nine o'clock that night. The family, or such part of it still on its feet, were just finishing dinner, cooked by Josephine, and in everyone's opinion a great improvement on whatever Berthe would have offered them.

It was Berthe whom he wanted.

'She's shut herself in her room and won't come out,' said Bernard, admitting him.

The Brigadier was not to be put off. 'Where is it?' he enquired, in a tired voice.

By this time, Josephine, Caroline and the Colonel had abandoned the table and were crowded at the dining room door.

'Up those stairs,' Bernard told him, indicating the flight rising along the inner wall.

Kergrist went up, knocked, received no reply, knocked again, announcing himself. Screams and shouts came from inside the room.

The four people waiting at the foot of the stairs exchanged glances.

'Don't ask me to reason with her,' said Josephine. 'Berthe wouldn't give me so much as the time of day.'

The men turned to Caroline.

'All right,' she said reluctantly, 'but don't expect too much,' she added, and climbed the stairs.

No amount of cajoling could persuade Berthe to open the door.

Brigadier Kergrist, who had had a long and trying day, lost patience. He came to the head of the stairs and looked down. He fixed on Bernard.

'I'm afraid I will have to force the door, Monsieur.'

'Is she that important a witness?'

'Yes, Monsieur.'

'Very well,' said Bernard. 'I'll give you a hand.'

With the Colonel at his heels, he ran up the stairs.

'Berthe,' he called out. 'We are going to break down the door if you don't open up. You can't stay there for ever.'

Inside the room the old servant went into hysterics.

Lottie appeared in the dining room doorway, roused from her drugged sleep by the din, and wearing a thick dressing-gown, which had suddenly become too large for her.

'What's going on?' she demanded, with something of her usual spirit.

They all tried to tell her, at once.

She held up a hand for silence. 'You need to interview Berthe, Brigadier Kergrist?'

'Yes, Madame.'

'Can't it wait until the morning?'

'No, Madame. I want a statement from her to place before Commissaire Orloff in the morning.'

'Who's he?'

'He will be taking over the investigation, Madame,' said Kergrist, his face wooden. 'Judicial police.'

Lottie thought for a moment, then, slowly, she mounted the stairs.

'Let me try.'

The men stood aside.

'Berthe!' Lottie let out a stentorian bellow. 'Stop that noise this instant!'

She could have been heard on the far side of a parade ground. An expression of astonished admiration appeared on the Colonel's face.

Overtopped, the screams inside the room died down, then stopped, replaced by heavy sobs.

'Now come out of there,' Lottie commanded.

That took a little longer, but at last a dull scraping informed those assembled on the stairs that a piece of furniture was being moved away from the door. A few moments later, Berthe emerged, sullen and fearful.

'There is nothing to be afraid of,' Lottie announced, being in full ignorance of the facts. 'The Brigadier wants to ask you a few questions and then we can all go to bed.' She glanced at Kergrist. 'I think I had better stay with her. We will use the library.'

She led the way, propelling the reluctant Berthe before her. The others trailed after her, only to be firmly excluded from the library by Kergrist.

'You have to hand it to Lottie,' said Josephine, collapsing into a chair in the drawing room. 'What a woman!'

'I find her rather terrifying,' said Colonel Clermont. 'I always did. Why do you suppose the police are so interested in Berthe?'

It was some time before they had an answer to that question. Strain their ears as they might, the few sounds – chiefly Brigadier Kergrist's voice or Lottie's – coming through the library door were too muffled to be made out.

Then Bernard was called in.

Another half-hour passed.

The library door was flung open. Berthe came through, closely followed by Brigadier Kergrist, who had her arm in a tight grip. Her face was set into lines of mulish obstinacy; his was of a man nearing the end of his tether. Without a word, he marched her through drawing room, dining room and kitchen and out to the waiting police car.

Bernard followed them. Of Lottie there was no sign.

Through the open doors came the sound of the car being driven away.

Bernard returned to the drawing room.

'The stupid woman won't say a word,' he announced. 'She'll have to spend the night in the cells. Lottie has gone back to bed. I suggest we all turn in, too.'

'But why should Berthe be so important?' Caroline asked,

unwilling to go meekly to bed with curiosity unsatisfied.

'Her lout of a nephew, Antoine, used to bring drugs to Estelle. Someone has blown the whistle on him, I don't know who. He seems to have disappeared, I gather, thanks to a warning Berthe sent to him last night.'

'That must be what Marie-France had found out,' said Caroline.

'It looks like it,' Bernard agreed. 'But if that is why Marie-France was killed, there must be more to it than that.'

'Estelle, too,' Caroline reminded him.

'Oh, yes,' said Bernard grimly. 'It occurs to me that it can't have been just a case of Estelle knowing too much about her drug supplier that made her dangerous to him. I think she must have been trying to use that knowledge. She was desperate for money. If she was willing to blackmail her own mother, would she hesitate to do the same to anyone else?'

Georges Quennec emerged from the warmth and company of Paul's bar into the bitter night air. He pulled up the collar of his coat to warm his ears. He had hung around in there for hours, listening to the speculations of half a dozen cronies. No one knew very much as yet, except the bare news of Marie-France's death and the launch of a murder investigation. Fantasies were more prolific than facts.

There was no sign of Chester Roach, who might have been expected to be propped up in his usual corner, drowning his sorrows. Georges had no idea if the American really cared for the girl, or was simply using her in some way. Whatever the circumstances, he must feel shock and some measure of grief, for a young life snuffed out.

He might need the presence of a friend.

His own loss still raw, Georges put off the moment of offering his services. He did not know if he could bear to witness another man's grief....

That night he drank rather more than usual, but gradually the voice of conscience became increasingly insistent. At last, he gave it best, wished Paul and the clientele goodnight and pushed open the outer door.

The quay lay silent under its load of snow, the river glinting darkly against the still whiteness. The sky was clear, the stars bright with frost. He huddled himself into his coat and trudged along, his boots blazing a lone trail.

He reached the place where the pleasure craft were moored. There were precious few at this time of the year.

One less than yesterday, in fact.

Chester Roach's boat had gone.

Chapter 5

Caroline came down early, thinking to start preparing breakfast for the household, with no Berthe to do it, being incarcerated in the cells at the Gendarmerie. On reaching the kitchen, she found Josephine there before her, and everything well in hand.

'You're incredible!' she said. 'They treat you like dirt in this house – let's face it, that's exactly how it is – yet when the chips are down, there you are, doing things for them. I don't get it!'

Josephine smiled.

'Call it salving my conscience. I am not proud of my part in all this. I let myself down when I fell for the temptation to get my own back on Lottie. Estelle brought me here for a very mean purpose. I should have let her get on with it on her own.'

Caroline laughed. 'Since when did either you or my mother refuse to dance to whatever tune Estelle chose to play?'

'I suppose you are right,' Josephine acknowledged. 'Poor thing!'

'Poor nothing! You both were silly with her. Somebody should have slapped her bottom at an early age.'

'You have a right to feel bitter towards her. Bernard tells me it was Estelle who came between you, last year. I didn't know that.'

'Ha!' Caroline snorted. 'I ought to thank her for that. She opened my eyes, that's all.'

Bernard put his head round the kitchen door.

'I'm glad to see that we do get some breakfast! I had no idea you were so domesticated, Mother. When I've stayed with you, there's always been some woman to do it all.'

'I run a business,' Josephine reminded him sharply. 'And I like things done properly.'

Bernard backed off. 'Anything I can do to help?' he asked humbly, and was handed a plate of bread to take into the dining room. 'And I owe you an apology, Mother. I phoned Father last night. He confirmed everything you told me.'

'Well, aren't you just a lawyer to the backbone,' Josephine snapped. 'Checking everything anyone tells you! What did you think I'd done? Made it all up?'

She slammed the lid of the coffee machine as if it had done her an injury.

Caroline, mystified but not daring to ask questions, snatched up the butter-dish and followed Bernard into the dining room. Colonel Clermont had come down, and had taken charge of the toaster. He was poking it fretfully. Lottie also was there, with a set expression on her face. Iron will had reasserted itself and Lottie de Saint Brieuc was determined to be her normal self or perish in the attempt.

'Berthe not back yet?' she barked.

Bernard shook his head. 'No sign of her, Aunt. I was thinking I should go into town to see what can be done for her.'

'You will do nothing of the sort,' Lottie shot back at him. 'I trusted her. She has been with me for over forty years. Yet she must have known that Estelle was taking drugs long before I did. She even knew how my poor girl was obtaining them. One word from her and the whole filthy business could have been stopped. But she kept her mouth shut. If that isn't treachery, I don't know what is.'

There was an awkward silence until Josephine walked in with the coffee. Lottie glowered at her old rival and was ignored. The Colonel fiddled with the toaster which was choosing that moment to assert the superiority of machines over their makers. A slice of bread was caught firmly in its grip and was burning merrily.

Josephine sat down. 'How is the General?' she asked nobody in particular.

Lottie glared down the table.

'Berthe—' she began, then stopped.

The Colonel fished out the burnt toast. 'I looked in on him about an hour ago,' he offered. 'He was still asleep.'

'Someone ought to go,' said Lottie.

'I will,' said Caroline quickly, and slipped out of the room.

She did not get far, encountering Léon in the anteroom. He looked worn and as if the long induced sleep had done him no manner of good. Together they went into the dining room.

The conversation at the breakfast table had returned to the subject of Berthe.

'She will have to go,' said Lottie. 'I suppose she must come back here to collect her things, but out she goes. I'll find someone else in the village.'

'Don't be too hasty,' Bernard warned her. 'You'll have a job to get a woman who will live in. And these days you can't just sack an employee on the spur of the moment.'

Lottie sniffed. 'Watch me! I will not have that traitor back here. Ah! there you are, Léon. How are you this morning?'

The General muttered that he was all right, a manifest lie, and sat down in his habitual place.

'I wonder when the new detective will show up,' said Caroline, having heard enough on the subject of Berthe and desirous of heading Lottie off, should she be thinking of going on.

'Commissaire Orloff,' said Bernard. 'Now there's a name to conjure with.'

'You know him?' Lottie demanded.

'I have heard of him. Very top level. I imagine that's your doing, Colonel?'

Clermont looked up from the toaster which was trying to burn the bread again.

'In a way. I did telephone my son,' he admitted.

'And Michel hauled on all the strings available to a Minister.'

'He has to protect himself. The jackals are always snapping at his heels,' said the Colonel unhappily. 'You know what the popular press can make out of the smallest whiff of scandal. He would like to have me out of here, but of course that isn't possible. Commissaire Orloff is being sent to wrap it all up, quickly and quietly.'

'Brigadier Kergrist didn't look very pleased at the prospect,' Bernard remarked. 'No love lost, I suspect, between the gendarmerie and the Judicial Police.'

* * *

Commissaire Maximilien Orloff came by helicopter, touching down on the football field, which did him no good in the eyes of Brigadier Kergrist. Ordinary policemen were obliged to travel by train. Half a dozen men who might have been better employed elsewhere had spent an hour clearing snow from the make-do landing strip.

The machine touched down, and a man jumped out, bending double as he ran clear of the whirring blades. Then the chopper was off again; the ex-passenger straightened up and a tall figure began striding over the frozen ground towards the waiting police car.

Brigadier Kergrist advanced to meet him. A big man himself, he was surprised to find himself topped by a clear six inches.

Orloff had a long face with high cheekbones and thick eyebrows over bright blue eyes. He lifted his hat to reveal springy light brown hair. He put out the hand not holding the hat.

'Brigadier Kergrist?' he said, in a deep incisive voice.

Kergrist, who sang tenor in the cathedral choir, put him down as a natural bass.

'Commissaire,' he replied politely, and discovered that the newcomer had a paralysing grip.

Kergrist put him in his late forties, but no bulging stomach marred the line of his heavy coat, which, like the trousers below it, the gloves, and the hat which the Commissaire was replacing on his head, looked very expensive.

The Brigadier thought he had never seen anyone who looked less like a French police officer. He nursed crushed fingers and it crossed his mind that a little of Commissaire Orloff went a long way.

He wondered what the Saint Brieuc family would make of him. Orloff could well be equal to Madame – in which case, he was welcome in Tremerrec.

The Commissaire expressed himself satisfied with the arrangements made for him at the gendarmerie, with the bare office, and the thick file on the desk ready for his attention.

An hour later he called the Brigadier in.

'Sit down,' he invited and Kergrist settled himself in the hard chair at the other side of the desk.

'Tell me,' Orloff went on, in his cultivated, upper-class voice. 'Before Georges Quennec appeared on the scene, were you satisfied that Estelle de Saint Brieuc was a suicide?'

Kergrist hesitated.

Orloff smiled. There was a beguiling quality to that smile, which transformed the stern features. The Brigadier thought the Commissaire knew exactly when and where to use it.

'Between these four walls,' Orloff added.

'No,' said Kergrist. 'I can't say that I, personally, was satisfied.'

'Why not? There was a history of threats of suicide, even one attempt, years ago.'

'The old servant, Berthe Guegan, didn't go along with that.'

'For what reason?'

Kergrist shook his head. 'I don't know. Getting anything out of her is like squeezing blood out of a stone. Maybe nothing more than pure contrariness. No hard evidence. Only dark hints.'

'You made a very careful examination of the scene of the fatality, and took a large number of photographs.'

'Routine, Commissaire,' said Kergrist, not without pride in the efficiency of his Force. 'We would have had a better chance if we had got to the body first. By the time the entire household had trampled over the ground, launched a boat and dragged the deceased out of the lake, there was not much left for us.'

Orloff sighed. 'I suppose it was a natural enough reaction to haul her out, if thoughtless. Especially when they had discovered that her bed had not been slept in.'

'Madame de Saint Brieuc,' said Kergrist, in a controlled voice, 'is a law unto herself.' As you will find out, he added mentally, with a speculative glance at the Commissaire.

'Did you consider the possibility that it might have been an accident?'

'I couldn't see why she went out into the garden. Quite a way, too. It is several minutes' walk to the lake. And it was a cold night.'

'She had drunk a good deal,' Orloff reminded him.

'So she fell over on the path. She didn't hurt herself much – just tore her stockings – but it must have shaken her. Yet she

88

still went on to the lake. It didn't make sense to me. I was hoping the pathologist might do a bit of unravelling.'

The Commissaire picked up the report on the autopsy, and leafed through it.

'There is no question that she drowned,' Kergrist went on. 'There are bruises on the body: on the legs and forearms, one at the back of the neck and a big one on the other side of the jaw. Some were made while she was alive, others after she was dead. There are both sorts on the legs and arms, the jaw bruise is definitely a post-mortem one, while the one at the back of her neck was caused before death. I had great hopes of that bruise, but it turns out that it isn't consistent with, say, someone knocking her out. Any or all of those bruises could have been made while she was in the lake. It hasn't been cleaned out in years. It is full of weed and broken branches.'

'There is usually buffeting in cases of drowning,' Orloff observed. 'And suicides have been known to change their minds at the last minute and thrash about trying to save themselves. Not to mention damage sustained through amateur handling by would-be rescuers.'

'All of which was pointed out to me,' said Kergrist bitterly. 'And with the General proclaiming his daughter a suicide, my hands were tied.'

'Quite so. The Saint Brieucs have been around here for a long time. I imagine pressure was brought to bear. The *juge d'instruction*? You don't need to tell me. So, in fact, you were quite pleased when Georges Quennec turned up, even though what he offered you wasn't really evidence at all?'

'Yes. Poor Georges! He is taking it hard.'

'Then let us see what we can do to ease his mind,' said the Commissaire. 'You have done a very good job, so far, Brigadier. The care that you took at the time of the first death, when no foul play was suspected, has preserved for us many details that otherwise might have been lost.'

Kergrist thought: he's a tactful devil, but that doesn't make him any less tricky. And I don't know what is his exact brief. Is he here to uncover truth or fix up an Establishment cover-up? 'Thank you, Commissaire,' he said.

Orloff rose to his feet. 'Shall we go to Keralic?' he invited.

* * *

A taxi brought Berthe back just after eleven. She poked her head round the kitchen door and was outraged to see the hated Josephine busy preparing luncheon.

'You get away from my sink!' she screamed.

'It's not your sink any more,' said Lottie, from the dining room doorway, drawn there by the sound of the departing car. 'Pack your things and go.'

Berthe stared at her. 'Go?'

'Yes. Go. I won't have you here.'

The old servant stood firm. 'You can't do that to me, Madame.'

'Why not?' Lottie demanded, red in the face.

'I haven't done anything.'

'Not done anything?' Lottie choked. 'You knew Estelle was taking drugs and you knew how she was getting them. Do you call that nothing? It was your duty to tell me.'

Berthe's face darkened in anger, so that she closely resembled one of the gargoyles decorating the flying buttresses of the cathedral. She glowered at her mistress.

'My first duty, Madame, was to my dead brother's son.'

'And what did you do for him, except encourage him to break the law?'

'It wasn't his fault that it was the only work he could find. Anyway, *she* got him the job.'

'What?' shrieked Lottie. 'Estelle?'

'That's right.' Berthe advanced on her employer until they were almost nose to nose. 'Your precious Estelle. It's her fault that my poor Antoine is being hunted by the police.'

Commissaire Orloff stood on the path leading down towards the lake. Narrow, with gentle curves, and overhung by trees and well-grown bushes, it followed the slope of the valley.

'This is a famous garden,' he remarked, looking about him. 'I have wished to visit it for a long time.'

Kergrist, who had already spent a good deal of time in the garden, under adverse conditions, was in no mood to appreciate it. He cleared his throat to recall the Commissaire to the business in hand. 'The snow has covered all the traces, such as they were,' he observed in disgust. 'But you have seen the photographs. She fell over here,' he added, indicating a spot a yard ahead of them.

'Over what?'

'Who knows? Her own feet, maybe, since she had been drinking.'

Orloff stamped his feet on the now well-trodden snow.

'How do you know it was here? I understand that it is only rough gravel. I couldn't see anything much in the photograph.'

'There wasn't anything to see. The gravel was scuffed up a bit, but not enough to signify. No footprints, of course. And in any case, lots of people were up and down this path when they found her in the lake. We only know that she fell here because there was a thread from her skirt caught in the lowest branch of that bush. I reckon she fell slightly sideways, where the path slopes down at the edge.'

'And how far is it from here to the nearest point on the lake?' the Commissaire enquired.

'Fifteen metres,' the Brigadier replied promptly.

He glanced sideways at Orloff, as if to say: make something out of that lot!

The Commissaire's gaze wandered back to the path, and the bushes overhanging it.

'That is a big strong rhododendron,' he remarked. 'There was no other trace of her clothing on that bush?'

'No. Not a shred.'

'What was she wearing?'

'A three-quarter-length fur coat, a woolly hat, gloves, boots. Underneath, a thick skirt and a woollen jumper.'

'What sort of boots?'

'Smart ones. High heels, soft leather. Came just over her ankles.'

'Hardly the right things to wear for tramping about a wet garden,' Orloff observed, and saw an expression of exasperation cross his companion's face.

Kergrist was kicking himself for having missed the point. 'You wait till you go into the house, Commissaire,' he said ruefully. 'There are enough rubber boots in there to set up a shop. No one goes out in the garden without them.'

'Yet Estelle did,' said Orloff softly. 'I wonder why.'

'If she was out to drown herself, it's neither here nor there. If she wasn't, then I would say she had no intention of moving off the path.'

'That is how I read it. Tell me, Brigadier, was that skirt and jumper what she had been wearing at dinner?'

This time, Kergrist felt a complete fool.

'I don't know, Commissaire,' he was obliged to admit.

'Then that is something we must find out,' said Orloff mildly. 'It looks to me as though she dressed up against the cold, so she had not popped out for a breath of fresh air for a moment.' He gazed across the stretch of snow which separated the path from the lake, broken only by luxuriant camellias, ready to herald the spring and halted by the unseasonable chill. 'Do we know where she entered the lake?'

Kergrist shook his head. 'There was no snow lying about at that time. The first fall had melted away days before. It is grass most of the way round. Kept mown in the summer, and still quite short. She was found near that little island.' He pointed to a low bank rising above the level of the lake. Bushes grew on it, and reeds. 'Pretty in the summer, that is, with lots of water fowl. She was found head first in those reeds. The inference is that she went in somewhere near here, and drifted across to the island, but if there were any traces on the bank they were obliterated by the clodhopping feet of the people who fished her out.'

'And they were?' asked Orloff.

'François Runan, the gardener – he found her and raised the alarm – and Colonel Clermont, assisted by Madame de Montigny and Mademoiselle Bracebridge. They had to launch the boat to reach her.'

'Why didn't she sink? One would have expected the body to go down to the bottom and not surface for some time. Is the lake shallow?'

'No,' said Kergrist, 'and it is full of weed which would hold on to the body. It was the fur coat that buoyed her up. Trapped air, I suppose.'

'So she was found straightaway. Or certainly within hours. I wonder how our operator liked that?' He gazed up and down

92

the stretch of water. 'How was this lake formed?'

'There is a spring at the top of the valley. It has been dammed in various places, to form pools and a canal, and this lake. It flows out over there into another pool and finally through the grotto to the river.'

'So there is a moving current. Which means, for Estelle to end up in those reeds, yes, indeed, she must have entered the water somewhere round here. Now, Brigadier, let us do a bit of reconstruction. We know something happened on the path. She fell down.'

'Or was attacked.'

'Exactly. The attack is a reasonable assumption. Now, she was quite a large woman. Not fat, but big-boned.'

'Took after her mother,' said Kergrist.

'I will accept your word on that. Now, how easy would it be to overpower her?'

'All the witnesses insist that she was drunk. So, not so difficult. But she had to be transported over those fifteen metres to the water. I doubt if she went of her own accord.'

'Carried? Dragged?' Orloff speculated. 'There must have been traces on the grass, but, as you say, too many people have gone over there since.'

'You would have thought, with a General and a Colonel about the place, that one of them would have thought of following the correct procedure,' said Kergrist, bitterly. 'I gather that Colonel Clermont tried, but naturally he was overborne by Madame de Saint Brieuc, who insisted that her daughter be brought out of the lake immediately. There was no suicide note, but they were all convinced that she had made away with herself. She had threatened it, on that last day.'

'So when did you begin to have doubts?'

'Not until I had questioned the servant. But she is hardly a reliable witness, as I have discovered since. Considering she had her nephew to protect, she was plain stupid to try to upset the suicide theory. I reckon she couldn't resist the opportunity to spite her mistress. I was the only one who listened to her.'

'All very convenient for our operator,' Orloff commented.

'However, there is no point in wasting time over that now. We must tackle the thing from the other end. Why was she murdered?'

'If we are to believe Georges Quennec, her own family got rid of her because she had stepped out of line. But he is obsessed, poor fellow.'

'Is he now? And where was he when Estelle was killed?'

'In Tokyo.'

'Good God!' Orloff exclaimed. 'That sounds like a cast-iron alibi. It will have to be checked, all the same.'

'The only other motive in sight is this drug traffic,' said Kergrist. 'Her family go for that.'

'They would, wouldn't they? It takes it right away from them. What do you think, Brigadier?'

'Chester Roach has gone missing,' replied Kergrist obliquely.

'Ah, yes! It is unlikely that we have two murderers running round Keralic. We must consider the two cases together. What about this American?'

'I keep my eye on what goes on in the port. We get all sorts of types here in the summer. Most of them are ordinary yachtsmen, but there is the odd one I am glad to see the back of. Roach sailed in last summer and stayed on. I can't say that we have anything specific against him, except that he has no visible means of support and private sailing boats have been known to carry other things than happy holidaymakers. Estelle de Saint Brieuc was receiving supplies of heroin from somewhere.'

'Would Roach have to use the boy Antoine as an intermediary?'

'We will soon know,' said Kergrist grimly. 'I think that silly mother of his has him hidden in the attic. I'll have him tonight.'

Caroline stood at the study window, peering out over the unbroken snow of the garden. Angled as it was in the tower at the end of the house, she had a view down the valley. There was no sign of life, but she knew that there were men going about unknown police business.

'Can you see them?' asked Bernard from a chair by the fire.

She shook her head. 'I wonder what they're doing?'

'Going over the ground,' said Bernard. 'Good luck to them, with this snow.'

She turned away from the window. The presence of the police spread a sense of unease throughout the house, and she was thankful for his company. Which was very odd, under the circumstances.

'Have you seen him?' she asked. 'Commissaire Orloff?'

Bernard smiled grimly. 'He'll be with us all too soon.'

'I don't think I have anything to tell him. Or you. You weren't even here when Estelle died.'

Josephine came in and dropped into a chair opposite her son.

'I have just escaped from the kitchen,' she announced. 'You wouldn't believe what is going on there. Lottie and Berthe are screaming at each other and I think every grievance from the past forty years is being aired. When I left, Lottie was accusing her of drinking the alcohol out of the preserved cherries. Crazy, the pair of them!'

Bernard stood up.

'I'll go and sort them out,' he said, and left the room.

'What's come over him?' Caroline enquired. 'He's diffe-rent.'

Josephine smiled. 'He is taking his position seriously, I should think. Charles must be the heir to Keralic now – and that means Bernard. There's a turn-up for the books, if you like!'

'I think it's all a nightmare,' said Caroline, in a small voice.

'It is, isn't it? I can't believe it's happening. First Estelle and now Marie-France. They can't have been murdered, can they?'

'Those policemen pounding all over the place seem to think so,' said Caroline, unhappily. 'I wish I could go home.' If there was a home to go to, she added to herself.

Josephine caught her thought. 'You come with me, when we are free to go.'

Caroline stared. 'Do you mean that, Josephine?'

'I know you feel badly about your mother. But she has her

95

own life to live, you know.'

'I suppose so,' muttered Caroline, gloomily.

'Alan is a decent sort of chap. It may work out wonderfully. And if it doesn't, you and I will have to pick up the bits. So we'd better stick together, hadn't we?'

'I wouldn't be in your way?' asked Caroline, hesitantly.

Josephine shook her head. 'Of course you wouldn't.'

'It is very good of you.'

'I need company as much as anybody else. With your mother remarried and Estelle gone, I am going to need you, Caroline.'

'What about Bernard?'

'Don't bother your head about him! I do what I please. He hasn't exactly been brought up to be fond of me. In any case, I have a feeling that, for once, he would approve of what I do.'

Caroline felt the blood rush up into her cheeks and said nothing.

Commissaire Orloff and Brigadier Kergrist had reached the grotto at the end of the garden. It was a square building of local stone, backed by a bank crowned with a grove of well-grown bamboo, now bent almost horizontal by the weight of snow. In front were two stone water-tanks, frozen over, with a set of stepping-stones making a causeway between them. Beyond that, the screen of trees which marked the boundary, a little tree-girt bay and the wide estuary.

A solitary gendarme, peaked with cold, stood guard at the open doorway in the centre of the building.

They picked their way across the stepping stones.

Kergrist addressed his man:

'Nip up to the courtyard, lad. It'll set your blood circulating again. Bring down the team so that they can number and dismantle anything the Commissaire wants taken away.'

The young man, glad to be relieved of his sentry duty, dashed off.

Orloff was examining the hinged iron grille which was the gate of the grotto. It was a strong, but delicately wrought, piece, ornamented with acanthus leaves. From it dangled a length of rope.

'No pretence about accident, this time,' he commented. 'I imagine that rope was attached to some specially weakened spot in the vault. I see the grille opens outwards. Very convenient. One tug on the gate and down the whole roof comes. But it takes a minute or two to do it. Long enough for the victim to walk inside.'

The Commissaire stepped over the threshold. The floor was heaped with rubble, the centre covered with a tarpaulin. From the walls, mermaids intricately fashioned from shells gazed down while high at the back a trickle of water fell from a spout festooned with icicles like frozen tears.

'How much of all this has been moved?' he enquired, tapping one foot against a fallen stone.

Kergrist followed him in, bent down and twitched aside the tarpaulin. Underneath were more stones, and the chalked outline of a body.

'Only enough to let the doctor get at her. Otherwise, nothing has been touched. How much of it do you want?'

'The lot, if you please. We must try to reassemble that vault. And all the loose mortar, too.'

The Brigadier suppressed a sigh. It would be a long job.

'There are photographs?' asked Orloff.

'Naturally, Commissaire,' replied Kergrist stiffly. 'They should be on your desk by now.'

'Good.' Orloff's eyes wandered over the ruined building. Then he stepped outside and surveyed the bank behind it. 'Access to the roof doesn't look difficult. The ground is a lot higher at the back. Damn this snow! It gets in the way of everything.'

'I'm told,' said Kergrist, 'that it is only a matter of two or three feet to climb onto the roof from under those bamboos.'

'She came here to meet her boyfriend, the American, Roach? Did he come?'

'Someone did. By boat, which was the way he always came, according to the Bracebridge girl. There was a trail through the snow, but with all the footprints destroyed. A branch dragged over them, by the look of it. It must have been Roach. And for my money, he was our anonymous caller, too.'

'Who took the call? Hasn't Roach got an accent?'

'Yes, he has,' said Kergrist. 'Very pronounced. And you would expect the telephone to magnify it. Yet the man who made that call spoke French like a Frenchman. I should know. I took that call myself.'

'So it wasn't Roach.'

'It must have been, Commissaire. He could hardly ask a friend to ring us up to tell us there was a dead body in the grotto at Keralic. Not if he wanted to stay out of it. As he must do, since he has cleared off. There are a lot of questions I should like to put to that young fellow.'

The family assembled for lunch, served by a sulky Berthe, still on the premises, despite her quarrel with her mistress. She muttered under her breath as she handed the plates, which sufficed to stifle all normal conversation.

'What are we going to tell this Commissaire Orloff?' said Lottie, suddenly, even silencing the grumblings of Berthe.

'What about the truth?' Bernard suggested.

She ignored him. 'It's important that we stick to the facts, without letting ourselves indulge in flights of fancy,' she went on, glaring at one and all. 'There is no need to air our personal differences. It is perfectly clear that poor little Marie-France was killed because she knew something about these drug pedlars, and it follows that Estelle died for the same reason. The Commissaire will not want to inspect the dirty linen of this family.' Her baleful stare flickered momentarily over Josephine. 'Do I make myself understood?'

No one was prepared to argue.

'I wonder if this Commissaire will be able to stand up to Aunt Lottie,' Caroline whispered to Bernard, as they left the table.

'It could be quite a battle,' he replied, with a grin.

Even as he spoke, someone knocked on the kitchen door. At the sound, everyone froze for a few seconds, then shuffled into the library where the coffee was waiting.

There was another assault on the big iron knocker of the outer door, longer and more impatient.

'Berthe must have gone to ground again,' said Bernard. 'I'll let them in.'

He headed for the kitchen, with Caroline at his heels. For some reason that she did not care to examine, she found Bernard's presence comforting, in this house of violent death.

He flung open the door. Outside stood a small knot of men: three gendarmes, Kergrist, impressive in his uniform, looking the embodiment of the Law, and a tall man in plain clothes, who stepped forward.

'Orloff,' he said, removing his hat.

They fell back before him.

'And you are?' he said.

Bernard pulled himself together. 'This is Mademoiselle Bracebridge. I am Bernard de Montigny.'

'Of course,' said the Commissaire, running his eyes over the pair of them as if he were committing them to memory, as indeed he was.

'Will you come this way, Commissaire,' Bernard went on. 'We are all in the library.'

Orloff's gaze travelled round the big square kitchen and up the stairs to where Berthe lurked suspiciously in the gloom of the landing. Then he stepped through the dining room door which Bernard held open for him.

He took in the dining room – like a walking camera, as Caroline described it afterwards – and after that the drawing room, missing nothing, from the disposition of the furniture to the smallest detail of the hunting scene on the tapestry on the wall. Then into the library, less imposing, even cosy if such a word could be applied to the splendours of Keralic, and the waiting family.

'Commissaire Orloff,' Bernard announced.

Lottie looked the newcomer over.

'I am Madame de Saint Brieuc,' she said, in exactly the right tone for addressing the tradesmen.

Behind the Commissaire, Caroline started to giggle, and she observed that Bernard's mouth twitched at the corners.

Orloff gave Lottie the camera treatment.

'Madame,' he said, indifferently, and turned to Léon, who was struggling to his feet, his face red with the effort and with shame at his wife's blatant rudeness.

'General?' said Orloff.

Léon offered his hand. 'May I present Madame de Montigny and Colonel Clermont?'

Everyone shook hands, except Lottie, who was trying to devise a way of looking down her nose at a man who was a great deal taller than herself.

'I am glad to find you together,' said Orloff, declining the offer of a seat. 'Please remain here. I wish to speak to you all—'

'We made statements to the local police,' Lottie cut in.

'I have read them, Madame,' Orloff replied frigidly. 'I regard them as discussion documents,' he added, crushingly.

Lottie subsided. 'As you wish,' she said. 'Please be quick about it. This is a house of mourning.'

'All in good time, Madame. First, I wish to inspect the belongings of the deceased ladies.'

Lottie opened her mouth to argue, but Léon forestalled her.

'Certainly, Commissaire,' he said quickly and with some of his one-time authority. 'We will wait here, at your convenience.'

By this time, Kergrist and his men were in the library, which they had reached in time to hear the exchanges between Lottie and Orloff. The Brigadier slipped round to the anteroom door, which he opened.

'This way, Commissaire,' he said, with a pleased expression on his face.

The party of policemen trooped into the anteroom.

'Well!' Lottie exploded, as the door closed behind them.

Her husband stared her down. 'I don't think I have ever been more ashamed of you,' he said icily, and she gaped at the unexpected rebuke. 'You can't class that man with the peasantry. What do you know about him, Bernard?'

'His background? White Russian descent, and out of the top drawer, I understand. But don't expect any favours from him just because he's one of us.'

'I can't imagine why a man of breeding should dirty his hands with police work,' said Lottie, in an attempt to stage a come-back.

100

'Orloff,' said Caroline. 'Wasn't that the name of one of Catherine the Great's boyfriends?'

Bernard shook a finger at her.

'Don't you dare ask him!' he said, with a grin.

Chapter 6

Their feet echoed along the tiled floor of the upstairs corridor. Windows on one side gave light, with oak doors, panelled and carved, opening off on the other. Kergrist came to a halt before one bearing official seals.

'This is the girl's room,' he said, and broke the seals to open up.

The room was dark, with strips of winter light round the edges of the shutters. One of the gendarmes crossed to the window and flung back the painted wooden panels.

Orloff advanced, gazing round. It was spacious, with a sloping roof and dormer window along the front, the curtains and bedspread in cheerful blue and white. A happy litter of clothes, tapes, records, make-up and magazines proclaimed the late owner's age and sex.

'I didn't find anything here,' muttered Kergrist, who had an eighteen-year-old daughter of his own. He could not help but think . . .

Commissaire Orloff, approaching the contents of the pathetic room with suitable detachment, also drew a blank.

'Nothing,' he said in disgust. 'That boyfriend of hers was careful not to commit himself to paper. *If* he was engaged in the drugs racket and *if* she knew enough to be dangerous, the knowledge died with her. All we have for certain is that she knew the boy Antoine acted as an errand boy. God knows if that's significant. Let's have a go at her mother's room.'

It lay at the other end of the corridor, next to that of Lottie.

'This was closed up only two days ago,' said Kergrist removing the seals. 'A case of shutting the stable door after the horse has bolted. I did a search the morning she was found – looking for a suicide note, of course – but I didn't see any need to seal off the room. I did it as soon as Georges Quennec had said his piece.'

Estelle's room was done out in yellow and white, with touches of pale green. There was a tester bed, flanked by delicate wall-lights, rich rugs on the floor, furniture gleaming with the care of centuries. An open door revealed a tiled bathroom.

'Quite a show-place, this house,' Orloff remarked.

'I don't know that I would care to live in a museum,' said Kergrist with a grin. 'I wouldn't dare put my feet up here.'

They started on a thorough search of the room. It yielded a lot of information about the late Estelle's choice of reading as a child, and a hoard of ancient birthday cards, photographs, theatre programmes and invitations, none of which appeared to have been disturbed for years. The cupboards were stuffed with clothes, many of outdated fashions.

'Did she ever throw anything away?' muttered Kergrist, groping in the back of the wardrobe.

Orloff was busy at an antique desk. Its fragile drawers were crammed with old bills, letters, chequebooks and bank statements. 'Only anything that might have been of use to us,' he said bitterly. 'All this rubbish tells me is that she threw money about in every direction, which we knew. What's that you've got?'

Kergrist held up the object that he had fished out from the back of the wardrobe. It was a red woollen dress, badly torn at the neck.

'What a waste!' he remarked, slinging it back. 'That thing must have cost a bomb.'

'I wonder what she did with the details of that house she was after,' said Orloff, closing the desk. 'She must have been in correspondence with somebody. Not a thing here.'

'There was no special reason for her to have been buying,' Kergrist replied, his head in the wardrobe. 'More likely to rent, if we are to believe that she was hard up.'

'According to that letter of Georges Quennec's, she was expecting the matter of the house to be settled quickly. There should be something,' Orloff persisted. 'And if she did happen to be buying, where was the money coming from?'

'Her mother.' Kergrist emerged from the wardrobe and started on a chest of drawers. 'Or courtesy of the illegal drug trade.'

The Commissaire grunted. 'And there is nothing much to help us in that direction, either. Only this diary with the initials A.G. at intervals. That must be Antoine Guegan. It looks as though supplies came every ten days. Those dates might be of use if the stuff was coming in by sea. Where are the clothes she was wearing when she died?'

'At the lab. They were to be released after the completion of the enquiry, but fortunately no one had collected them. They're going over them again.' Kergrist slammed shut a drawer. 'There's damn all here.'

'I didn't expect to find much,' Orloff replied calmly. 'Anyone could have got in here in the days between her death and the funeral.'

'I doubt if outsiders could sneak in,' said Kergrist, surprised. 'There's always someone about the house.'

'I wasn't thinking of outsiders,' said the Commissaire.

The atmosphere in the library was hardly convivial. Coffee was drunk in a grim silence, which became the more suffocating when there were no cups to occupy idle fingers. Berthe swept in and removed the tray almost before the last drop was drunk.

'I thought you had given her the push, Aunt,' said Bernard.

Caroline, sitting next to him on the sofa, poked him. This was no time to be stirring the pot.

Lottie gazed at him malevolently. 'I have.'

'But Berthe won't go,' said Léon, in a sudden spurt of revolt against his domineering wife. He appeared to be enjoying the situation.

'Standing on her rights, is she?' Bernard enquired, ignoring a second poke.

'She will go,' said Lottie, 'once the police are out of the house.'

No one offered to challenge that. There was a long silence, with every ear stretched for sounds from above.

'They're taking their time,' said Lottie, in a tetchy voice. 'I can't imagine what they think they'll find.'

104

'For all our sakes, it is to be hoped that they'll come across something that will lead to the people who supplied Estelle with drugs,' said Bernard.

'What difference does it make to us whether they do or not?' Lottie replied, intent on putting him down.

'They might start looking closely at us, Aunt, if they don't,' said Bernard, silkily. 'They know we weren't one big happy family.'

'Rubbish!' Lottie snapped. 'Estelle was behaving abominably but that would have been sorted out.'

'You mean, you were going to give in?' Léon exclaimed.

'I would not receive that butcher's boy here,' said Lottie, grimly, 'but I doubt if Estelle really wanted that at all. She was after an income to support the pair of them. She would not have needed it if they were going to live here. And she brought over from England Josephine' – she all but choked at having to speak the hated name – 'to make sure she would get it.'

'And you were prepared to give it to her?'

'Yes, Léon, I was.'

'Did you tell her that?' Bernard enquired.

A spasm passed over Lottie's face. 'I hadn't got round to it. I was waiting for her to ask me again.'

Commissaire Orloff and Brigadier Kergrist descended the wide staircase.

'That door on the left,' said Kergrist, who was explaining the layout of the ancient manor, 'leads to the General's rooms.'

He crossed to it, flung it wide, to reveal a tiled corridor with high windows along one side.

'Bedroom, bathroom and study here, Commissaire. Corresponding upstairs with the bedroom of Marie-France, the little guest-room where Mademoiselle Bracebridge is sleeping, and the Colonel has the room over the study.'

Orloff looked back across the anteroom. 'Where does that lead?' he enquired, nodding towards a door on the other side, where the tower joined the main part of the house.

'That's the flower-arranging room.'

They crossed the grey-flagged floor to reach the unobtrusive door, half-hidden by the rise of the staircase. Kergrist opened it and they peered inside. It was a small place, no more than eight feet square. There was a workbench, with a large plastic bin beneath it, shelves furnished with an assortment of vases, a small sink, and another door with rusty hinges.

'That's an outer door, but they don't use it, Commissaire,' said Kergrist, but Orloff had already turned away.

They walked down the length of the anteroom, to the tall double doors which gave onto the library and the range of rooms beyond.

'It's quite a simple layout, once you have the hang of it,' the Brigadier went on. 'Houses this old grow, as people add on rooms over the centuries. All the main rooms lead out of each other, and in the rest of the house the rooms are at the front, with connecting corridors at the back.'

'It is very well kept ,' Orloff remarked. 'The garden, too. An interesting collection, botanically speaking.'

'The General's parents laid it out, sixty or seventy years ago. Madame is the gardener, these days. She is over eighty, but amazingly energetic.'

'Strong, too?' suggested the Commissaire in a reflective tone.

Kergrist shot him an interested glance. 'I wouldn't be surprised,' he said, and opened one of the double doors.

If there was a conversation going on in the library, it died in mid-sentence. Six pairs of eyes fastened on the Commissaire.

'My apologies for keeping you waiting,' he said, without much pretence at sincerity. He singled out Léon. 'General, I need to go over all the statements made by your family and guests. I am sure you would prefer to stay here rather than attend my office in town. Is there a room I may use?'

'This one, if you wish, Commissaire,' said Léon instantly. 'We can move into the drawing room, next door, and then you may call us in as you please.'

Orloff inclined his head. 'Thank you, General. But first,' he added, as everyone with the exception of Lottie began to rise, 'I wish to speak to all of you together. Please sit down again.'

They obeyed, while Orloff organised chairs for himself and Kergrist. He pulled out a notebook.

106

'Now, ladies and gentlemen, I will start with the murder of Estelle de Saint Brieuc. Is it correct to call her by that name?'

'Yes,' said Léon. 'My daughter resumed her maiden name after her divorce.'

'Thank you. I would like to piece together exactly what happened the evening she died. The medical evidence suggests that she had been in the lake for some hours before she was found. Therefore, I am assuming that she was killed before midnight. Now, all of you, except Monsieur de Montigny, were here that night. Let us begin when you assembled for dinner. What time was that?'

'Seven-thirty,' said Lottie. 'Dinner is at eight. I try to serve meals promptly, but someone is always late. It was Marie-France, that night, dolling herself up to go out as soon as she had bolted her dinner. I think everyone else was down by half past seven. For the *apéritif*, naturally.'

Orloff made a note. 'Who served the drinks?'

There was a short silence.

'I think I did,' said Colonel Clermont.

'So you did.' Léon nodded. 'I must say, Edouard, you do make yourself useful.'

'Does this matter?' demanded Lottie, impatiently.

'I am interested in your daughter's degree of drunkenness, Madame. It could have a material bearing on the manner of her death. Everyone who made a statement to Brigadier Kergrist mentioned that Estelle de Saint Brieuc had been drinking. So how much did she drink that evening?'

There was another silence.

Josephine broke it. 'I'll admit it has been puzzling me, Commissaire. Estelle really was drunk that night, but I don't remember her having more than two drinks before dinner and no one had any afterwards. There was some wine with the food, but I don't think she had more than the rest of us. She did drink rather a lot, and she could hold it, so –'

'Trust you to try to make yourself interesting!' Lottie cut in, blisteringly.

There was a brief uproar, while everyone tried to quieten Lottie or encourage Josephine, or both. Commissaire Orloff sat back and enjoyed it.

'If we might proceed,' he said, as the noise died down. 'Can anyone confirm Madame de Montigny's estimate?'

'Yes,' said Caroline. 'Now I come to think of it, Estelle didn't seem to drink more than the rest of us. But she certainly was high by the time we left the table.'

'Colonel,' Orloff invited. 'You poured the drinks before dinner. How many did she have?'

The old man frowned. 'I think Madame de Montigny is right. Only two. As we all did.'

'And what was she drinking?'

'Sweet Martini, as far as I can recall,' he said, and looked round as if appealing for corroboration from the others.

'That's right,' said Caroline, feeling someone ought to support the old boy. 'I was sitting next to her, and I remember wondering how she could bear anything so sweet. The rest of us were on Campari.'

'So,' said Orloff. 'She had two Martinis before dinner and a normal amount of wine. How many bottles were opened?'

'Two,' said Lottie, impatiently. 'Commissaire, there is no mystery about this. My daughter had been drinking in her room before she came down.'

'There is no alcohol in her room now, Madame. Has it been removed?'

Lottie stared at him. 'How should I know? I haven't been in there since—' she broke off, clamping her lips together.

Orloff glanced round the ring of faces. 'Has anyone raided that room for a spot of liquor?' he enquired.

No one wanted to answer that question.

Brigadier Kergrist rose to his feet.

'I'll ask the servant,' he said, and slipped out of the room, leaving a difficult silence behind him.

He returned quickly, spoke quietly to the Commissaire, and resumed his seat.

'Your maid says she went into that room only to close the shutters,' Orloff told them.

'Of course she had a bottle in her room,' Lottie insisted. 'There is no other explanation of her condition. One of the gendarmes must have taken it,' she added, glaring at Kergrist.

'Madame,' said the Commissaire sternly. 'I must ask you to keep to the point. If you wish to make accusations, Brigadier

Kergrist will escort you to the Gendarmerie and you may make them there.

Lottie tried to stare him down, and failed. She said nothing.

'To resume,' Orloff went on. 'It would appear that the deceased drank a good deal during the course of the evening, some of it in private, so that by the time dinner was over, she was drunk. What happened after dinner?'

No one appeared anxious to tell him.

'My daughter made a scene,' said Léon, with dignity, and sorrow. 'It was very embarrassing. Then she went upstairs. We thought she had gone to bed.'

'Do you know what time this was?'

The General shook his head. 'Not really. It must have been towards ten o'clock. What do you think, Edouard?'

'About that,' the Colonel agreed. 'It spoilt our evening, Commissaire. Madame de Saint Brieuc went to bed shortly after. The other ladies followed her. The General and I talked for a few minutes, then we, too, turned in.'

'And where was the daughter, Marie-France?' asked Orloff.

'Out with that dreadful American,' said Lottie. 'She did not come in until nearly one in the morning.'

'You heard her?'

'I sat up for her,' said Lottie, grimly.

Commissaire Orloff seized on the point.

'So, in fact, Madame, you were up and awake. You were listening for your granddaughter. What else did you hear?'

Lottie gave a little shrug of her shoulders. 'People were moving about the house for a while. I heard someone go down.'

'Your daughter?'

'Not then. I know the sound of her door.'

'Which is next to yours,' said Orloff, reminding himself.

'That is correct, Commissaire. It was one of the other rooms.'

'I went down about eleven,' Caroline offered, and at once felt guilty.

'Thank you, Mademoiselle. Did you see anyone?'

'No. But all the lights were on.'

'And you came straight back up?'

'Yes.'

'Berthe had instructions to leave the lights on for Marie-France,' said Lottie. 'By my husband's wish. I thought it was a waste of electricity.'

'Did you hear your daughter go down?'

Lottie's shoulder sagged suddenly.

'Yes. Twice.'

'Twice? At what times?'

'The first time would be after eleven. She came back up again about twenty minutes later. To fetch something, I suppose, because she was in her room only for a few minutes. Then she went down again.'

'And what else did you hear while you were waiting? Or did you doze off?'

'Yes, I dozed. The penalty of old age, Commissaire. But not for long. I was awake again at a quarter after midnight. I thought I might have missed Marie-France, so I went along to her room, but she wasn't there. As I told you, she came in at one.' She passed a hand over her eyes. 'I said a lot of harsh things,' she added, with uncharacteristic softness.

'Thank you, Madame. I have one more question for you all, ladies and gentlemen. What was Estelle wearing that evening?'

The men looked blank.

'I can tell you that,' said Josephine, with the ghost of a smile. 'A red woollen dress and a pair of rather pretty high-heeled ankle boots.'

The drawing room had taken on the atmosphere of a dentist's waiting room. They sat round in a strained silence as first Lottie, then the General, followed by Josephine, were called into the library. None of them reappeared.

'It's like a sausage-machine,' said Caroline, as Josephine went through the double doors, leaving herself and Bernard the sole occupants of both the room and the sofa.

'They don't want us all hashing it over amongst ourselves, until they have had a go at us first,' said Bernard. 'What's the matter?'

'I find that man frightening.'

'Who? Orloff?'

'Yes. He has an aura of power about him.'

110

Bernard wondered if she realised just how much she might have to fear – and how best to convey a warning.

'A most formidable person,' he agreed, in a neutral voice.

'Who – and what – is he?'

'Someone very special. He keeps in the background, but he has a reputation. He's given delicate jobs to handle discreetly. It's only because of the Colonel that he's been sent to us. Otherwise, we should be subject to normal police procedure, like ordinary citizens of the Republic. Believe you me, we should be given a rough ride. Orloff wears kid gloves, figuratively speaking.'

'But these crimes are nothing to do with us, except that the victims are ours.'

'The notion that both Estelle and Marie-France were killed by drug traffickers is a most appealing one,' Bernard admitted. 'But don't imagine that Orloff will accept it just like that, and not look elsewhere. Estelle must have made enemies in her rather erratic career.'

Caroline shook her head. 'Bernard, that won't do. It doesn't offer any sort of explanation of the killing of Marie-France. It isn't as though mother and daughter were very close. They fought non-stop. The only connection is the drug business. Estelle went out that night to keep an appointment. It must have been with one of those men.'

'I wish I could be so sure.'

'Look, she'd changed her clothes. If she'd gone out for a stroll she would have slipped on a coat. Nothing more. But she took off her dress and put on a skirt and jumper. To keep warm. Doesn't that suggest that she thought she might be hanging around outside for some time? Bernard, the Commissaire is onto it. He was asking what she wore. And I know it because I was there when she was brought out of the lake.' Her face paled at the recollection and her voice shook. 'I saw her. I'll never forget that!'

An arm came round her shoulders and she felt herself drawn into a comforting nearness to a warm body.

'Don't take it to heart, old girl,' he said in a brotherly tone.

Caroline's pulse raced. She discovered that she did not feel *sisterly*. Without thinking, she snuggled closer, and the arm tightened.

'Bernard?' she said, wonderingly, and looked up at him. The look on his face made her heart turn over. There was nothing brotherly about it.

The library door was flung open.

'Mademoiselle Bracebridge, if you please,' said Brigadier Kergrist.

Caroline jumped up. The door closed behind her.

'Blast!' said Bernard de Montigny.

Georges Quennec was ushered into Commissaire Orloff's office at the Gendarmerie. He went in warily. All Tremerrec knew that a special detective of high rank had been sent from Paris. As might be expected when a family such as the Saint Brieucs was involved.

One glance at the Commissaire and one word from him confirmed Georges in all his preconceived ideas.

The Saint Brieucs belonged to the ancient royalist aristocracy which could maintain itself only by being a closed society. One of their own kind had been sent to their aid.

This man had come, not to investigate, but to hush up.

Georges was aware of Orloff's scrutiny, taking in his shabby clothing and his big rough hands with their broken nails.

'Monsieur,' the Commissaire began, 'I know this is painful for you, since it was the death of your fiancée that started this investigation—'

'Not so painful as to know she is unavenged,' Georges broke in.

'I can understand how you feel, Monsieur.'

'Can you? I doubt it. You can't fool me. I know why you're here.'

'Do you indeed?'

'Yes, I do!' Georges cried, furiously. 'You are here for a cover-up. So that that lot – the Saint Brieucs – can get away with it.'

'No one is going to "get away" with anything, if I can help it,' said the Commissaire coldly. 'I am aware of your accusations against the Saint Brieuc family – I do not doubt that they treated you badly – but let us see what substance there is behind your allegations.'

'You've read Estelle's letter?'

'I have.'

'Would you expect the woman who wrote that letter to commit suicide a few days later?'

'No, Monsieur, I would not.'

'That's something, I suppose,' said Georges, bitterly.

Orloff regarded him with a measure of compassion.

'From the evidence of that letter, Monsieur, I would say that she was trying to make a fresh start, even if she was going about it in a somewhat original fashion.'

'What do you mean by that?'

'Extortion, Monsieur.'

'The money would have come to her anyway. Would it matter if she wanted it in advance?'

'Quite. Yet you are convinced that some member of her family contrived her murder.'

'Not for the money. Family pride, Commissaire. She was letting the side down by marrying a peasant like me. Her mother calls me "the butcher's boy".'

'Very impolite. It may interest you to know that Madame de Saint Brieuc was prepared to give her daughter the money.'

'She can say that now that it's too late!'

'On condition that you lived elsewhere,' Orloff added.

Georges laughed bitterly. 'Estelle and I would never have lived at Keralic.'

'It is a place of outstanding beauty. I should have thought it would appeal to an artist.'

'I would have suffocated. But thank you for allowing that I am an artist. It makes a change from being a butcher's boy.'

'I went to that exhibition of yours in Paris last year.'

Georges stared in surprise. 'Did you? It didn't exactly take the art world by storm. I sold a few pieces, but we only just about broke even by the time we had paid for the room and the publicity and made good the damage that those kids did – climbed all over some of the pieces while their silly mothers watched. Said they thought it was an adventure playground.'

'Most regrettable,' said Orloff, with a straight face, but with a gleam in his eye.

'I suppose modern sculpture does look a bit like that,' said Georges, reluctantly. 'I was mad at the time. Estelle came to that show.'

'She was interested in art?'

'Not she! My poor Estelle was an ignoramus. She was

dragged along there by a friend. She was bored stiff and started talking to me for something to pass the time. She hadn't a clue who I was. Not until I started dragging those kids off my stuff. She was terribly embarrassed because she had not been at all polite about my work. She insisted on taking me out to lunch to make amends. We never looked back, though you'd have thought we'd have no common ground at all.'

'Tell me about her. Had she enough resolution to make a fresh start?'

'With my help, yes, Commissaire.'

'Even to finish with drugs?'

'She was going to take a cure after we were married. She had already cut down on drink. She promised me she would never take more than two *apéritifs* and two glasses of wine with her dinner.'

'You know what evidence on that score was given during the initial enquiry?'

'Yes,' said Georges sadly. 'I really thought she would keep that promise.'

'One witness says she seemed excited. Perhaps that was why she slipped. The tone of her letter confirms that. Victory over her mother was in sight. And she was arranging for a house. What do you know about that?'

'The house?' Georges repeated, blankly. 'Nothing much. She said it would be a surprise. It was somewhere in the Midi. Well away from Keralic and Tremerrec. It doesn't matter now.'

'It might. It depends upon who was paying for it.'

'I don't understand.'

'Two people have been killed at Keralic, Monsieur,' said Orloff patiently. 'The inference is that the murders are connected. The only clear link is the matter of drugs. Estelle was an addict and Marie-France knew how she received her supplies. Estelle was desperate for money and was applying pressure to her mother to give her some. Could she not also have been using her knowledge of her suppliers of heroin to provide a bit extra – say, to buy a house?'

Georges shook his head. 'You'll never convince me. Marie-France was killed for the same reason as her mother.'

'Her association with the undesirable Chester Roach? One thing about that interests me greatly, Monsieur. Under the circumstances, I would have expected her mother to be sympathetic. Yet all the witnesses insist that Estelle was violently opposed to Roach. Do you know why?'

'That was the only subject we ever quarrelled about,' said Georges, his face set into lines of pain. 'Chester is a pal of mine. Estelle couldn't stand him. She would never tell me why.'

'You know he's disappeared?'

Georges nodded unhappily.

'Tell me, Monsieur,' Orloff continued. 'Did you ever ask yourself if Roach really is an American?'

Georges stared at him. 'He spoke with an accent.'

'But otherwise his French was good?'

'Perfect.'

'And how did he manage to live? He didn't have a job.'

'I don't know,' Georges admitted uncomfortably. 'I never asked.'

'And do you know where he might have gone?'

'No, Commissaire, I haven't a clue. And I don't think it matters, either. You don't have to look outside the walls of Keralic to find your murderer.'

Caroline had persuaded the General into looking over what there was of his book. He sat in his armchair in the study and dutifully started reading through the pages of the typescript. After half an hour, he pushed it aside.

'It's no good, my dear,' he said gently. 'I can't concentrate. See if you can find Edouard for me, there's a good girl.'

Caroline slipped out of the room.

The old man sat staring into the fire. So this, he thought, was how it felt to have come to the end....

His eyes closed and his head dropped forward in the easy slumber of age.

The opening door woke him.

'Is that you, Edouard?'

'No. Bernard. May I come in?'

Léon opened his eyes. 'Of course, my boy. Sit down. It's time you and I had a talk.'

Bernard took the chair at the other side of the fireplace.

'It seems a bit inadequate to say how sorry I am about Estelle and Marie-France.'

'It's the end of the family, Bernard. No more Saint Brieucs at Keralic. It will be up to Charles and you now. I don't know how you will manage. Lottie's money will go back to England. You could not be blamed if you sold Keralic.'

'No!' said Bernard, quickly.

A small flame leapt into the old eyes. 'So you care a little?'

Bernard nodded. 'I always have. Since the first time I was permitted to come here.'

'That pleases me,' said Léon simply. 'You know the truth, don't you?'

'I do. Mother has told me. Rather reluctantly.'

'Do you mind?'

'That you are my father? I think I knew it a long time ago. There is the portrait.'

The old man smiled. 'A son in my own image. Every man's dream, I suppose.'

'Embarrassing for you.'

'For poor Lottie, mainly. Bernard, there is nothing I should like more than to acknowledge you.'

'You can't do it. There are too many people to hurt.'

A mischievous smile touched the General's lips. 'I rather hoped Estelle might do it for me. You know why she brought your mother here?'

Bernard sat up. 'That was a bit wicked of you, wasn't it?'

'Oh, it's worse than that. I might as well make a clean breast of it. I did my best to stiffen Lottie's opposition. I tried to make her call Estelle's bluff – only I knew it would not have been a bluff. There was a time when I thought I had pushed it all too far, and that I was responsible for poor Estelle's death. I am glad I don't have to live with that any more. And I hope they find those drug suppliers very quickly.'

The clothing was laid out on Orloff's desk: skirt, jumper, fur coat, gloves, stockings, boots. Expensive stuff, now fit only for the ragbag. The Commissaire hovered over it. On the other side of the desk, Kergrist leafed through the laboratory report.

'I wonder why she went out in those boots,' said Orloff, picking one of them up.

'They were all right as long as she stuck to the path.'

'Rough gravel? Not good going for a tipsy lady in the dark.'

'She fell over,' Kergrist reminded him.

'So she did. That drunkenness bothers me, Brigadier.'

Kergrist frowned. 'I wish we had found a bottle in her room. There must have been one.'

Orloff looked up. 'You're worried by Madame de Saint Brieuc's allegation against your men?'

'Damn right I am.'

'What are you doing about it?'

'What do you think? I'm turning this place upside down. If one of them did lift that bottle, I'll find him.'

'I shouldn't spend too much time on it, if I were you,' said the Commissaire, unexpectedly. 'There are more important things to do. What sort of weather was it the night Estelle was killed?'

Kergrist drew a deep breath to control a spurt of temper. He understood all too well that Orloff accepted that one of his men had removed that bottle. Not waste time on it, indeed! The resentment against an outsider being sent in over his head welled up again. 'Cold. Wet. No snow,' he said tersely.

'I think we must have all that snow cleared between the path and the lake. The ground underneath must be frozen hard by now. We might pick up a few traces. Will you set some men onto it?'

'Yes, Commissaire. Right away.' He made for the door, but could not resist adding, 'A lot of feet trampled that ground. It was one big muddy mush.'

Orloff glanced up. 'Yes, I'm sure it was,' he said with a hint of that smile. 'What I want to look for is a trace of these boots. These sharp little heels would have dug holes in sodden grass – if she walked, or was conscious when she was dragged.'

Kergrist nodded and went out, admitting reluctantly to himself that the clever devil had a point there.

When he returned, Orloff was still examining the boots. Kergrist asked himself what was the difference between doing that and reading the laboratory report, where every scratch was listed.

'The men will go over to Keralic first thing in the morning, Commissaire. The light has nearly gone today. Will that do?' he asked, a shade anxiously. He would not put it past this hot-shot detective to demand arc-lights.

'Perfectly, thank you. She put up a bit of a fight, didn't she? These boots are scuffed.' He dropped them and picked up the gloves. 'These, though, look quite new and untouched, apart from water damage. The stockings are torn.'

'When she fell over,' said Kergrist.

'And landed in that bush. I wonder why she didn't put out her hands to save herself?'

'Someone else was holding them? Behind her back, say?'

'You could be right, Brigadier.'

'There were bruises on her wrists.'

'Quite. And on her arms, too. Our operator must have had a good grip to bruise the flesh through the thickness of that coat,' said Orloff, picking up one fur sleeve and squeezing it. Then he looked at it more closely. 'There is a small bald patch here, Brigadier. Did we find a tuft of fur?'

'No, Commissaire,' Kergrist replied firmly, glad to be sure of something. What was the man getting at?

'Now, what does all this tell us?' Orloff murmured, gazing down at the clothes.

'That she dressed up warmly to go out,' Kergrist offered, stifling impatience at the obvious question. 'She would not have bothered changing if she was just popping out for a breath of air to clear her head. I can tell you something else, too, Commissaire. She was in a hurry.'

Orloff looked at him keenly. 'How do you make that out, Brigadier?'

'She was wearing a red woollen dress that evening. There was only one dress answering that description in her wardrobe. And I found it stuffed in the back of the cupboard. She was in such a rush to take it off that she tore it.' Kergrist glanced at his watch. 'Do you mind if I go, Commissaire? I reckon it is just about the right time to drop in on Madame Guegan – she'll be home from work now – and pick up that young rip, Antoine.'

'Certainly, Brigadier,' Orloff replied. 'We want that young

118

man. I think I will go to Keralic. I'd like to take a look at that dress.'

Josephine knocked on Lottie's bedroom door, and was bidden to enter.

Lottie was sitting at her desk, a heap of papers before her, but doing nothing. She stared at her visitor in surprise tinged with outrage.

'What do *you* want?'

'I wondered if there was anything I could do for you.'

The colour rushed up into Lottie's face. 'You? No, there is nothing you can ever do for me. Go away!'

Josephine retired hastily, in the face of such a rush of venom. She turned to see her son emerging from his room further along the corridor.

'What are you doing, Mother?'

She smiled ruefully. 'I extended an olive branch. And got my hand bitten off.'

'Lottie won't give in. It is her rage that keeps her going.'

'I'm sorry for her. She's lost everything now.'

'She won't thank you for your pity,' said Bernard, as they started down the stairs. 'Mother, you knew Estelle better than anyone. How far was she into drugs?'

'Far enough to need help. Give the despised Georges his due. He had persuaded her to take a cure.'

'Is it possible that she could have known enough to be a danger to her suppliers if she chose to talk?'

Josephine hesitated. 'That is important, isn't it?' she said, at last.

'The whole present theory of the murders rests on it. But put that out of your mind, Mother. Give me an honest assessment.'

'But I just don't *know*, Bernard. There is one thing, though,' she added, as they reached the hall. 'That boyfriend of Marie-France, Chester Roach. Estelle had met him somewhere. Before she came back here and found Marie-France involved with him. She was very upset when she discovered who this marvellous boyfriend was. Do you think he could have been involved with drugs?'

119

'Have you told the Commissaire this?'

'No. Should I?'

'You should indeed, Madame,' said a deep voice, and Commissaire Orloff emerged from the growing shadows of the anteroom.

Josephine was surprised into a squeak.

'Oh! I didn't know you were here!'

'You are just the person I wish to see, Madame.'

Josephine clutched at Bernard's arm. 'Really?' she said faintly.

Orloff smiled at her and she blinked.

'I need your assistance. Will you come upstairs to Estelle's room and show me the dress she was wearing that last evening?'

'Of course,' said Josephine, uncertainly, and turned back to the stairs.

Orloff followed her, with Bernard, determined not to miss anything, close behind.

Josephine opened Estelle's wardrobe.

'I can't see it here,' she said blankly, gazing along the crowded rail of coathangers.

'Try the back, at the bottom,' Orloff recommended.

Obediently, Josephine dived into the wardrobe.

'I've got it,' she said, backing out. 'Oh, but it's all torn!'

Orloff took it out of her hands, and carried it to the window to get the best of the failing light.

The tear started at the side of the neck, and reached a foot down the front. But it was not only the rent that had spoilt the dress. The fine red wool of the bodice was marred by a large stain.

CHAPTER 7

Antoine Guegan was a small, plump, spotty youth with a pair of eyes that bolted round the hard faces of his captors and appeared to be on the point of popping out of his head. He kept on thinking that it was all a bad dream and in a moment he would wake to find himself safe in the snug little hideaway in the attic. *Maman* had assured him that the police would never think of looking for him under his own roof. But they had, and it was no dream: he was sitting on a hard chair in a bare room with barred windows.

Large tears began to roll down his fat cheeks.

'I don't know anything, I really don't,' he babbled, for the umpteenth wearisome time, as if mere repetition would carry the day. 'You fellows shouldn't pick on a poor boy who was only trying to earn a few francs now and then. I don't know—'

Orloff turned away.

'I'm beginning to believe him. Can't you shut him up?'

'*She* got me into it. Madame Estelle,' the querulous voice insisted. 'She told me what to do. Where to go to pick up the packet. She—'

'Most of the time we have a job to persuade them to talk,' said Kergrist ruefully. 'Shall we leave him to cool off in the cells for a while?'

'By all means. Any news of Roach?'

They went back to Kergrist's office. A young gendarme followed them in.

'Message just in, sir,' he said, placing a typed sheet on the Brigadier's desk.

Kergrist glanced at it.

'The boat has turned up. In Guernsey. No sign of Roach.' He sighed. 'That means extradition. If he has not gone straight to the mainland, Gatwick or Heathrow, and from there anywhere you please. But I shall go on looking for him.'

'There is something not quite right about Roach as a drug smuggler, murderer or murderer's accomplice.'

'He is the only candidate we have, so far,' said Kergrist, thinking that it was not always a virtue to look beyond the obvious. One could be too devious and expect everyone else to be likewise.

Orloff shook his head. 'I don't fancy him as our operator. For instance, that phone call you received. You thought he made it, Brigadier, for all that he did not speak with an accent. I agree with you. There is no one else. One set of tracks from the bay to the grotto and back, with a branch dragged over them to make sure we could not match footprints to any identifiable boot. Otherwise, the snow unbroken. I take it your men were careful not to mess anything up?'

Kergrist gritted his teeth. Then his better judgement told him that it was a fair question.

'They were careful, Commissaire. I was with them myself.'

'I didn't doubt it, Brigadier. Now, one can understand him obliterating the tracks—'

'And taking off—' Kergrist put in.

'Exactly. Wanting absolutely nothing to do with the investigation of the death. Which is not the usual behaviour of either an innocent member of the public or a man whose girl has just been killed. But it doesn't make him a murderer or an accomplice, for that matter.'

'So what does it make him?'

'That is the interesting point. And there is more, Brigadier. Why phone you? She would have been found sooner or later. Even more peculiar: why did he leave the rope in position on the iron gate? If he rigged up that trap himself or knew that one of his friends had done so, surely he would have removed that rope, which gave away the whole thing. Roach had been hanging round Marie-France for months and meeting her regularly at the grotto. He must have known about that roof. Without the evidence of that rope, no one would have doubted that the collapse of the vault had been anything but an accident.'

'There are bound to be other marks,' said Kergrist. 'The mortar must have been chipped away.'

'Agreed. And we shall find those marks now that we are looking for them. But it all comes back to that phone call. It looks to me as if Friend Roach was making sure that you would arrive at the scene of the crime before the alarm was raised at the house. As, indeed, you did.'

'Yes,' said Kergrist, thoughtfully, kicking himself for being a thick-headed country bumpkin. But was Orloff refining too much on what might still have been an ordinary reaction to finding Marie-France dead?

'Innocent men don't run,' he added.

'I need to know a whole lot more about Roach,' said the Commissaire. 'The only people who might be able to help are that lot at Keralic. I think I will go and spoil their evening *apéritif* for them. When am I likely to have a report on that dress?'

'I sent a motor-cyclist over with it, and the technicians at the lab are going to work overtime. Your name works wonders.'

Orloff's rare and winning smile appeared. 'I expect they want to pack me off back to Paris as quickly as possible,' he said, moving towards the door.

Kergrist felt the blood rise into his face. He was glad that the Commissaire walked out of the office without looking back.

Odile Quennec was beginning to wish that she had not come. Georges was being unreasonable, and while pouring it all out on her might provide him with considerable relief, it was doing nothing for her. She found his obsession with the Saint Brieuc family depressing. More, it was worrying. She was sure it could lead to mental breakdown.

'I might have known they would find a way of fixing the police,' he said, pacing about the studio. 'That Commissaire may spout a lot of fine words, but all he is going to do is pin it on poor old Chester Roach, or "person or persons unknown", and that will be the end of it.'

'Georges, stop it! You are driving yourself – and me – mad. No matter how much the Saint Brieucs disapproved of you and Monsieur Roach, it is crazy to imagine that they would kill Estelle and Marie-France to stop them marrying the pair of you. And Monsieur Roach has gone off in a very suspicious fashion. Even you must admit that.'

'He didn't want the police poking their long noses into his affairs. That doesn't mean he had anything to do with either murder,' Georges replied impatiently.

'So you admit he is a shady character!'

'Cut out the bourgeois morality, Mother. People have to earn their living as best they can these days.'

'So that is why you are half-starved?'

Georges stopped in his tracks. 'What's that?'

'Honest artists can only scrape a living. Dishonest ones make forgeries and fortunes.'

He stared at her. 'What has that to do with Chester Roach?'

'I am only thinking it out in terms of my bourgeois morality, of which, let me tell you, I am proud. I don't expect you to stoop to debase your own work, so don't you ask me to lower my standards. That Roach is at best a layabout, at worst a bad lot. You are so obsessed with the Saint Brieucs that you won't believe that anyone else could possibly be responsible for Estelle's death. And let me tell you that I think Monsieur Roach is a whole lot more likely to be a murderer than a pair of very old people who are trying to hold on to the dignity and honour of their family.'

Georges shook his head at her.

'I don't believe it! Mother, you don't know how the world works now.'

'I know how Tremerrec works. That is what people are saying.'

'They don't know what they are talking about.'

'Then tell them! If you want to clear your friend's name then you should give the police every scrap of information you have.'

'Waste of time! They don't take any notice of gut feelings,' Georges declared. 'I have a better way of doing it. One of these days, I'm going to Keralic to force the truth out of them.'

Berthe opened the door to Commissaire Orloff.

'What do you want at this time of night?' she demanded

truculently. 'Have you come to arrest me for drinking the juice out of the cherries?'

Orloff ignored the bizarre question and asked for Madame de Saint Brieuc.

'She is dressing for dinner. It is seven o'clock. Why don't you work normal hours like everyone else?'

She stepped back, ready to slam the door in his face.

The Commissaire put a large foot on the step. It was many years since he had been obliged to resort to such measures, which were far beneath his dignity.

Berthe eyed it and the heavy oak door. She prepared to test the resistance of his shoe.

Josephine, looking into the kitchen to make sure that dinner was being prepared, came to his rescue.

'Don't keep the Commissaire on the doorstep, Berthe. Let him in.'

The old servant glared at her. 'We don't want him,' she objected.

'We have no choice in the matter. Berthe, Madame will be very angry.'

'Madame is always angry,' Berthe retorted. 'The way she is going on about those cherries is something chronic. It is the excuse.'

'For what?'

'For giving me the push. Stealing, she calls it, just so that I can't have the law on her for wrongful dismissal.'

'I am sure you are mistaken,' Josephine said firmly. 'I doubt if Commissaire Orloff has come to question you about the cherries. Have you, Commissaire?'

'No,' he said, with a surprising hint of laughter in his voice.

'All right, then.' Grudgingly, Berthe moved back slightly. 'Come in.'

She retired, muttering, to the sink.

Josephine took Orloff into the drawing room, and settled him in a comfortable chair. Considering his importance, he had taken Berthe's treatment remarkably well. She hoped it meant that he was in a good mood, because there was no denying that his sudden reappearance at this hour was disquieting.

'I'm so sorry,' she apologised. 'There is a running fight

125

going on between Berthe and Madame de Saint Brieuc.'

'About cherries?'

'That is only part of it. Madame is furious because Berthe knew that Estelle was taking drugs – brought by the wretched Antoine – and did not tell her. She doesn't want Berthe here any more, though goodness knows where she would find another who would anywhere near replace her. And she doesn't want to find herself being sued. After all, Berthe has been here for over forty years.'

'I fail to see where the cherries come in.'

Josephine laughed. 'It is quite ridiculous. Two bottles of preserved cherries are dry. I expect the seals are faulty and the alcohol has evaporated. Madame de Saint Brieuc will have it that Berthe has drained it off and drunk it. On that subject, Commissaire, am I allowed to offer you a drink?'

Orloff shook his head. 'No, thank you, Madame. This is not a social call.'

'You are working late.'

'On a job such at this, Madame, I prefer to work all hours. Until it is finished.'

'That sounds rather frightening, Commissaire. Whom do you wish to see? Not everyone is here. Bernard has taken Caroline out for the evening. I hope there won't be any more snow.'

He looked across at her. A handsome woman, by any standards. In the light of a lamp near her shoulder, her hair turned to a deep shining bronze. He wondered what the General thought of her now.

'You are worried about your son, Madame?'

Josephine laughed and her face glowed.

'One does not bother one's head about Bernard. He can take care of himself. And of Caroline. Mind you, it might do the pair of them good to be snowed up in a car.'

Orloff grinned. There was a refreshing quality to this woman.

'Do they need that? Being done good?'

'I thought they were going to make a match of it, last year. But something went wrong, and then it was all off.'

'Why was that?'

'I don't know,' said Josephine, and suddenly remembered that Estelle had had a hand in it. She flushed at the thought that one more unwary word could have set her on a slippery slope.

The Commissaire noted the rising colour. It improved her looks.

'Estelle, I imagine?' he said. 'Or Marie-France?'

A look of horror came over Josephine's face. 'Are you a mind-reader?'

'No, Madame. You are not a good liar.'

'I don't know if that is a compliment. It was Estelle, but I honestly have no idea what she did. And that *is* the truth.'

Lottie came in and looked very put out when she perceived Orloff.

'What do you want now?'

'Whatever I deem necessary to my investigation, Madame,' he replied, sternly. 'Please sit down.'

Lottie eyed him with disfavour, but said nothing. She took a chair as far from him as she dared.

'Would you like me to go?' Josephine asked.

'On the contrary, Madame. I wish to talk to both of you. On the subject of Chester Roach.'

'I have already told you all I know,' said Josephine. 'Estelle let it slip that she had met him, but she clammed up about it straightaway. I couldn't get a word out of her on the subject again.'

'What's that?' said Lottie, shooting a venomous look at her one-time rival. 'That is the first I have heard of it.'

'Why did you think Estelle was so against Roach?' Orloff asked her.

'Marie-France was too young to entangle herself,' said Lottie, promptly. 'We knew nothing about him: he had no job, no means of supporting her.'

'Those sound like *your* objections to him, Madame, rather than your daughter's.'

'No, Madame is right,' said Josephine. 'Those were exactly the arguments Estelle was putting forward.'

'Strange,' commented the Commissaire, 'when one considers her own history.'

'It is not strange for a mother to want to protect her daughter from making the mistakes she made herself,' said Lottie, in a dogmatic tone.

'You had seen Roach for yourself, Madame?'

'Only from a distance, Commissaire,' said Lottie, disdainfully. 'Marie-France tried to persuade me to see him. I refused.'

Orloff turned to Josephine. 'And you, Madame?'

'I admit I was curious about him. I went down to the port one morning, and happened to meet him as he was walking along the quay.'

'Did you get a good look at him?'

'Yes. He passed right by me.'

'And what did you think of him?'

Josephine paused.

'Caroline insists that he is older than he says. I think she is right. He makes out he is in his early twenties. I would put him at over thirty. Of course, he dresses young.'

'Did you hear him speak?'

'Not on that occasion. The following day, I met him and Marie-France in the town. I stopped and she was obliged to introduce us.'

'And what language did he speak to you, Madame? English?'

'No. French. With an accent that even I could detect.'

'But you accepted that he was an American?'

'I did,' Josephine admitted. 'Isn't he?'

'It seems to me,' said Lottie suddenly, 'that, for once, my daughter was showing some sense. Who is this Roach? Is he the one who killed my girls?'

'At this stage, Madame, I am not in a position to tell you.'

'Have you caught that wretch Antoine?'

'Yes, Madame, he is in the cells now.'

There was a loud howl of anguish from the other side of the door to the dining room.

In a few strides Orloff reached it, the women at his heels. He flung open the door in time to see Berthe disappearing through the kitchen door in the opposite wall. A strong smell of burning filled the air.

'There goes our dinner!' Josephine yelped, dodging round

128

Lottie and the Commissaire with the agility of a rugby forward, and plunging through the dining room and into the kitchen.

Caroline and Bernard had escaped to Lazardrieux. They sat in an almost empty dining room, looking out through plate glass over the darkling river. On the opposite bank lighted windows shone yellow onto the snow and street lamps brightened the frosty air.

'How pretty!' she exclaimed.

'It's lovely on a long summer evening,' said Bernard, his nose already in the large menu. 'What has come over this place? I have never heard of these things.'

'La Nouvelle Cuisine, Monsieur,' murmured the waiter, hovering at his side.

Bernard let out something between a moan and a growl, and started a lengthy inquisition as to the composition of these unknown dishes.

The food, when it arrived, was as pretty as the view. Bernard complained that he preferred taste to presentation.

'What you want are rich sauces and cholesterol disasters,' said Caroline, nibbling at a collection of almost raw vegetables arranged as a flower.

'That's right,' he admitted cheerfully, prodding an un-peeled prawn as if it were his worst enemy.

'It's an improvement on Berthe,' Caroline suggested.

He laughed. 'You're right there. She's always been the same. She and Lottie have bickered for forty years.'

'It's a real fight now.'

'They'll calm down. I don't think either could do without the other.'

'Your mother is holding Keralic together at the moment,' said Caroline.

'Amazing, isn't it? She is made of much sterner stuff than I thought. Imagine coming back to the place at all, and then standing in as a ministering angel. She is passing up a wonderful opportunity for revenge. What is this muck?' he added as the waiter placed another fancy plateful before him.

'Do shut up, Bernard. He'll hear you.'

'I hope so. What is France coming to?'

129

Caroline giggled. 'Well, I'm enjoying it. Thank you for bringing me, Bernard.'

'I have been trying to get you to myself for days.'

Caroline's attention was suddenly fixed on her plate. 'Really?'

'Yes, really. And you know it. Caro, last year – what is it you insist on calling it?'

'The awkwardness.'

'As good a description as any, I suppose. Very awkward for both of us with our mothers living in each other's pockets. I made a bloody fool of myself.'

Caroline forced herself to look out of the window. Her heart was beating wildly, but she reminded herself that she must take it slowly.

'Yes, you did,' she agreed. 'Of me, too.'

He winced. 'I deserve that. Look, can't we make a fresh start?'

Nervously, one of her fingers drew a pattern on the tablecloth. Play it cool, she told herself.

'Last year,' she said, 'you made it perfectly clear that I was not the sort of person you wanted as a wife. The woman you were looking for must be able to advance your career in some way. By influence or a lot of money or both. All I am likely to inherit is the family property, where my father is presently struggling to make ends meet. I don't know if it's that he's a bad farmer or that the land is useless. It's not exactly profitable and I doubt if anyone would be mad enough to buy it.'

Bernard groaned. 'That was last year! Until you came up on my horizon I thought that was what I wanted. Then when you got all upset over that other thing—'

'And shouldn't I have done? I'm not willing to share you with another woman, Bernard!'

'It wasn't like that! Estelle was telling you a big tale for the sole purpose of playing a dirty trick on me. There wasn't a word of truth in it. Estelle detested me.'

'Why didn't you explain?' Caroline demanded.

'Because I was a bloody fool!' said Bernard soberly. 'I thought I saw a way of escaping from you, and going on with my plans for my life and career. But it didn't work, because I discovered that there is no one else in the world who will do. I have tried to forget you, Caro, but I can't do it. Then when I arrived at Keralic and found you there! I know I am asking a lot, but I love you and I beg of you to give me another chance.'

She turned her face towards him. 'If you really want it,' she said softly.

'I do,' he said, and reached out for her hand.

In the twinkling of an eye, their corner of the restaurant turned into a small piece of Paradise. The river glinted solely for them, and the bright stars of winter were theirs alone.

'I suppose,' said Bernard, reluctantly, some time later, 'that we had better go back, much as I dislike the idea. What I would prefer to do would be to get in the car and drive as far away as possible.'

Caroline giggled. 'Aunt Lottie would disapprove.'

'Let her!'

'But, Bernard, we can't!'

'No, more's the pity. Come on!'

She picked up her handbag. 'It's been wonderful to get away for a few hours.'

'Is that all you think?' he demanded, with mock severity. 'What about us?'

'That's different. What I meant was—'

'I know. It will all be over soon, Caro.'

'I hope so. The Commissaire unnerves me the way he keeps popping up.' She clutched his arm. 'Bernard! Look!'

He followed her gaze. In a far corner, a man and woman appeared to be having a very enjoyable dinner *tête-à-tête*. They were sharing a joke, and their laughter held an intimate quality.

'Talk of the devil!' he gasped. 'But whatever is my mother doing dining out with Orloff?'

In the clear grey light of morning, a group of gendarmes toiled in the garden at Keralic. With the aid of blowtorches, as well as picks and shovels and elbow-grease, the stretch of rough grass between the path and the lake was cleared of snow. Underneath lay an unsavoury mess of churned-up mud. The men stood clear, hot from their labours. Orloff and Kergrist moved forward.

The Brigadier looked down on the half-frozen morass. This had to be a waste of time.

The Commissaire had in his hand the photographs taken at the time that Estelle's body was pulled out of the water. He began comparing them with the newly revealed traces in the mud. It was a long process. The men, chilling rapidly, stamped their feet and flailed their arms to keep the circulation going in their bodies. At last, Orloff snapped his fingers and one of the gendarmes handed him a sheet of plastic. He spread it on the ground at the side of the mess of tracks, and knelt down. Kergrist, feeling it was required of him, joined the Commissaire. Together, they pored over the muddy grass.

'Boots everywhere,' said Kergrist in a depressed voice.

'That must be the boat,' Orloff pointed to a clean clear line. 'Nothing but a straight piece of wood could make that mark. But there isn't a trace of a hole made by a smart little boot with slender high heels, is there?'

The Brigadier was obliged to agree.

'So,' the Commissaire went on, 'Estelle did not walk to the lake. Nor can she have been conscious if dragged. Had she been, she would have resisted, dug those heels in.'

'She was carried,' said Kergrist, striving to keep the impatience out of his voice.

Orloff rose to his feet. 'She was tall. It would take one large man or two smaller ones to carry her.'

'That's right,' said the Brigadier, all too aware of his men, bored and cold, listening for a good reason for all the shovelling and effort.

'We are making progress,' said Orloff, and someone hastily suppressed a snigger.

The Commissaire ignored the small sound and returned to the path. He stopped in front of the large rhododendron.

'Now, we know that she fell into the bush, but did not try to save herself.'

'Someone knocked her out and she fell forward,' Kergrist suggested.

'Possibly. Next point: where is her torch?'

The waiting gendarmes stopped fidgeting.

'Her torch?' said Kergrist.

'She would hardly have been prowling about the garden on a dark winter's night without one,' observed Orloff mildly. 'There is no torch among the exhibits collected from here. So where is it? Of course, there may be an ordinary explanation: someone could have picked it up. So let us find out if they did.'

Rapidly, the Brigadier detailed men to search the area, to go to the house, to round up all those gendarmes not present who had set foot in Keralic.

'In case,' he explained bitterly to the Commissaire, 'one of them pocketed it, like that blasted bottle!'

They walked slowly up the path.

'Suppose we don't find that torch,' said Kergrist, after a while. 'The killer could have taken it.'

'Indeed he could, but he must have had one of his own to find his way to their rendezvous in the first place.'

'He might have chucked it in the lake,' said Kergrist, gloomily, envisaging a lengthy and messy dragging operation.

They trudged over the snow, packed hard by the passage of many feet. Another dreary thought entered the Brigadier's head: how long would it be before the Commissaire required every scrap of snow clearing away from this path, down which Estelle must have walked in those fancy boots?

The house loomed up ahead of them, the steep roofs glistening white against the grey sky.

'Is that torch important, Commissaire?'

'I don't know,' Orloff replied. 'It is a little detail, that's all. I make a habit of following up details, Brigadier. One in a hundred pays off.'

Bernard discovered his mother sitting peacefully in the library, reading.

'I was wondering where you were this morning,' he said. She looked up. 'You know I never come down to breakfast.'

'What were you doing dining out with Commissaire Orloff last night?'

Josephine's eyes gleamed with amusement.

133

'Am I accountable to you, Bernard?' she teased him. 'If you must know, Berthe burnt the dinner.'

'So Orloff kindly took you out and fed you. Why you? What happened to the rest? Starvation?'

'It was kind of him,' she replied calmly. 'I organised soup and eggs for Lottie and Léon and the Colonel. Berthe shut herself in her bedroom and wailed. Poor old things, they are not in good shape. They are too old to cope with the horrible shocks we have had to endure.'

'It was a fairly horrible shock to see you in that restaurant!'

'Didn't you and Caroline want to be seen together?' she asked mischievously. 'How indiscreet of me to appear at the wrong moment.'

Bernard frowned. 'Mother, this is not funny.'

'I should hope not,' she replied, enjoying herself at his expense. 'Are your intentions honourable? I shouldn't like to think that Caroline was being led astray.'

'I have every intention of marrying Caroline,' Bernard said stiffly. 'What did Orloff want? I don't suppose he took you out for the pleasure of your company.'

'Thanks a bunch!' Josephine exclaimed, nettled.

For a long moment, mother and son glared at each other. Then a reluctant grin dawned on Bernard's face.

'I'm sorry, Mother. Am I behaving like a stuffed shirt?'

'You are! It is high time some woman took you in hand. I am so glad that you and Caroline have settled your differences.'

'And Orloff?'

She laughed. 'I found him an entertaining companion. But I don't flatter myself that he gave me a slap-up dinner—'

'Slap-up? With that fancy chef in the kitchen?'

'You and Commissaire Orloff should get together. I enjoyed the food. I also have no doubt that I was pumped very expertly.'

'To what end? I thought the police were looking for drug pedlars? Or do you know more about that than you will admit to the rest of us?'

Brigadier Kergrist made his way to Orloff's office. The Commissaire was engaged on the telephone, but waved him to a chair. Kergrist sat down and listened to an unenlightening half of a conversation.

Soon, Orloff put down the phone. 'We may forget about Chester Roach.'

Kergrist could scarcely believe his ears. 'What?'

'Roach is not our operator. I put through an enquiry last night, Brigadier. That call was the response.'

'Who was it?'

'Someone I know in Narcotics,' said Orloff. 'Roach is one of their boys.'

Kergrist stared. It was a jolt to have a prime suspect whisked away from under his nose. But it explained certain anomalies.

'So he is not an American?'

'No. But he has spent a lot of time in the United States, and can pass for one.'

'I suppose his name isn't Roach, either.'

'I doubt it,' Orloff agreed.

'Why did he run? All he had to do was show some identification and we would have left him alone.'

The Commissaire smiled. 'Don't take this to heart, Brigadier, but those fellows trust no one. Not even fellow-cops. What I am telling you now is in the strictest confidence. Just between the two of us.'

'Yes, of course, Commissaire, but I don't understand.'

'Roach was here on a job. However, it's not finished and he could not afford to risk blowing his cover. He reported the finding of Marie-France to his own superiors before he phoned you. They ordered him out of Tremerrec on the instant.'

'If he was here on a job,' said Kergrist, thoughtfully, 'that means they may be running the stuff in through the port.'

'That was Roach's theory. Based, I gather, on the fact that he met Estelle de Saint Brieuc in some doubtful company in the Midi some months ago. I think that explains Estelle's violent opposition to her daughter's attachment to Roach. He was posing as a user, and she had no reason to suppose that he was shamming. Be that as it may, Estelle was the only lead they had to this particular operation, so Roach sailed up the river, struck up an acquaintance with Marie-France, and sat

135

down to wait for her mother to show up and, hopefully, lead him to her suppliers.'

'And did she?'

Orloff shook his head. 'Roach came to the conclusion that Tremerrec was clean, and so was Estelle, apart from the minor offence of possessing heroin. He had identified Estelle's source of supply, but it is no more than a postbox. He was just about to move on elsewhere when Estelle was murdered.'

Kergrist digested this. 'So we're barking up the wrong tree, are we? She wasn't putting the bite on any drug trafficker. And she wasn't killed to keep her quiet.'

'That's how I see it,' said the Commissaire. 'The whole case hinged on Roach being either the murderer or an accomplice. Most particularly in the murder of Marie-France, since that depended upon his date with her at the grotto.'

'You don't seem very surprised, if I may say so.'

'I can't say that I am, Brigadier. The angle had to be investigated thoroughly, but I didn't fancy it, right from the start. There was a time element in the murder of Marie-France that bothered me. Berthe's message to her nephew – the warning that Marie-France knew about the delivery of drugs to her mother – didn't go out until early evening. It would require quite an organisation to set that trap at the grotto ready to catch her at ten o'clock the following morning. Not to mention the fact that it was snowing hard all night.'

'We've been wasting our time,' said Kergrist, bitterly.

His tone implied: and you let us do it.

'Not at all,' said Orloff cheerfully. 'Everything has to be chased up. You know my principle: investigate every last detail. You have also been very useful to me. While our operator has been sitting back, enjoying the spectacle of you busily going in the wrong direction, I have been pursuing some enquiries of my own, very quietly.'

Kergrist felt the by now familiar surge of resentment. He did not like being used, even in the course of justice.

'Is there any word from the laboratory?' the Commissaire enquired.

'About the dress? The analysis of the stain is done. The

report is being typed now. They will send it over by special messenger as soon as it is ready.'

Orloff grunted. 'I am more interested in the grotto roof at the moment. I want to know how it was made to collapse, how much technical know-how would be required, and how much strength would be needed to rig that trap.'

Kergrist looked surprised. 'Strength? You mean, could a woman have done it?'

'I keep an open mind. Some women are a lot stronger than they look.'

Kergrist wished he could do a bit of mind-reading. There were four women at Keralic. Had the Commissaire his eye on one of them?

'We have found Estelle's torch,' he said, happy to be able to announce a success.

'Where?'

'In her own bedroom. The old woman, Berthe, is prepared to swear that it is the only one she had, since Estelle had asked her for one only the week before. What we haven't been able to find is anyone who will admit to coming across it in the garden and putting it back in the bedroom. The only prints on the thing are those of Estelle and Berthe.' Kergrist hesitated, torn between pride and honesty. Honesty won. 'I can't make anything of this, Commissaire. It seems daft. She must have had a torch. No matter how well she knew the garden, walking in the dark on a rough path is tricky.'

Orloff smiled, and immediately the Brigadier felt less of a fool, illusory though he knew it to be. He wondered if the Commissaire smiled when he made an arrest.

'Then let me help you. She was dressed to stand around in the cold, but she didn't change her smart boots. Now if she intended to walk in the garden that seems odd. Then there is the matter of the torch. The evidence suggests that, strange as it may seem, she did not take one with her. No one has come forward to say she borrowed theirs, nor would she need to, when she had one in her own bedroom. Yet if she was going as far as the lake she would certainly have to have a torch. Therefore, she was not intending to walk to the lake, but to some place where she would not need a torch.'

137

'But where—' Kergrist began, and stopped short, baffled.

'She intended to remain near the house, where there is no rough walking and where all the lights were left burning for the convenience of Marie-France coming home late.'

'Then how did she get into the lake?'

'She may have walked to her death,' said the Commissaire, 'arm-in-arm with her killer, who would have a torch, of course.'

'That sounds very matey,' Kergrist observed.

'I expect it was, if that is how it happened.'

'Then she must have known her killer.'

'Undoubtedly. Look at the motives, Brigadier. Once one removes the bogey of desperate drug traffickers, what is left? I don't accept Georges Quennec's ideas on how far the Saint Brieucs would go to protect the family name. Yet two women have been killed, and I refuse to accept that there are two different murderers. So what links them? Land and money. Both were heirs to Keralic and the fortune that supports it. So who comes in for that inheritance, once Estelle and Marie-France are out of the way?'

CHAPTER 8

The General's sad old eyes fixed themselves on some faraway object, visible to him alone.

'I was afraid of this, Commissaire,' he said quietly. 'It seemed such a wonderful release when it looked as though vile drug pedlars were responsible. Dealers in death, those men. The murders of my poor girls did not seem so monstrous when they were at such hands. But now it has all come to us again. It is my duty to answer all your questions. What do you want to know?'

Orloff gazed at him with compassion. They were in the study, all very formal, with the General seated behind his desk and himself in a chair at the other side.

'The succession,' he said, 'to the property.'

'There are two separate inheritances, Commissaire. From the two families. The house and estate are on the Saint Brieuc side. I can tell you only about that. The money comes from the Bracebridges. You will have to ask my wife. I may say that I would never have been able to maintain Keralic without Lottie's money. The Saint Brieuc heirs won't come in for a penny of it.'

'And who are those heirs?'

'My half-brother Charles de Montigny and his son Bernard. I imagine you know the truth about Bernard's parentage, but we must continue to maintain the fiction. It is a small consolation to me that eventually my own son will succeed here.'

'And can the de Montigny gentlemen afford to keep up the estate?' Orloff enquired.

Léon shook his head. 'I very much doubt it. I am afraid they will be obliged to sell. Our mother – Charles's and mine –

was an heiress, but my father spent most of her money on Keralic, so she didn't have much to bring to her second marriage. Not that it would have made much difference. Charles has no head for business. Money runs through his fingers.'

'And Monsieur Bernard?'

'He is entirely different,' said Léon, with ill-concealed pride. 'I understand he is making an excellent living, but I have no idea if it would stretch to keeping up Keralic.'

'Would he want to?'

'You will have to ask him that yourself, Commissaire,' said Léon, refusing, despite all the dictates of duty, to voice his personal opinion that Bernard would like nothing better. 'Is there anything else?'

Orloff shook his head. 'Not for the moment, General. You understand that we may be working in the garden for some little time yet. We have taken away, for examination, the fallen stones of the grotto roof. They will be returned eventually, but if we are able to bring someone to trial – as I trust we will – those stones will have to be submitted as evidence.'

'I am not very concerned about that roof now,' said Léon. 'Nor the grotto. I don't think I will rebuild it. Not after poor little Marie-France met her death there. That wipes out all the old memories.' He sighed and seemed to look for a swift moment into some private place. 'Josephine and I used to meet there.'

Orloff rose. 'Thank you, General. That will be all for the moment. Now I need to see Madame de Saint Brieuc.'

'She is waiting for you in the library.' The old man glanced round the study at the piles of papers and notebooks laid out on a table at the far side of the room. 'She never comes in here. Sometimes, it seems to me that it is a mirror of our life together. She lives in the rest of the house. The whole of my life is here, in those papers and diaries. I am supposed to be writing my memoirs, you know.'

Orloff wandered over to the table. Each pile of papers was labelled with the name of a place or of a campaign, from Léon's time as a cadet at St Cyr to his retirement, full of honours. It read like chapter-headings in a history book – and

140

this man, weak and old now, had marched and fought his way through it all.

'It should make interesting reading, General.'

'I am not getting on with it very well,' Léon confessed. 'It is much more difficult than I had imagined. One can express one's exact opinion of the dead, but what about the living? Has one the right or the duty to tell a truth which will harm the living or expose an evil that is beyond remedy?'

'Memoirs that do not reveal secrets are rarely interesting,' Orloff observed.

Léon smiled. 'That is very true. Perhaps I am being chicken-hearted. The truth may be that I don't want to write this book at all. Even reading through my old diaries has brought back things best forgotten. Living through those times was bad enough. Living through these times is not so good, either,' he added, wryly.

'The end of all this may very well be one of your truths that harm the living,' said the Commissaire. 'The evil is already beyond remedy. There remains only justice.'

Colonel Clermont came across Caroline and Bernard in the drawing room.

'I thought you would be working, Caroline,' he said. 'Léon has shut himself in the study.'

'Commissaire Orloff is there with him,' she replied. 'I don't know if that augurs fresh horrors or if he is just reporting progress.'

'If any,' Bernard supplied. 'Drug dealers are slippery customers. Or so I am told. Anyway, Uncle Léon is unlucky in his assistants. Estelle jacked up the work. And Caro here is going to be married. As soon as possible,' he added, putting a proprietorial arm round her shoulders.

A smile lit the Colonel's worn features.

'That's wonderful news. My congratulations to both of you. So one spark of good has come out of all this evil.'

'I hadn't thought of that,' said Caroline, 'but you're quite right. It was only Estelle's death that brought Bernard here. Otherwise, we might never have met again.'

'Oh, I don't know,' said the Colonel. 'There's a pattern to these things, only sometimes we can't recognise it. The main

141

point is that you have come together, and I hope you will have a long and happy life before you. Once this is all over,' he added, and the shadows seemed to close in upon them once more.

'If it ever is,' said Bernard, gloomily. 'If the murders were committed by these drugs boys, even the famed Orloff might not be able to catch them. They were mighty quick off the mark in silencing Marie-France, and from what I can gather, they left few clues behind them. They'll be out of the country by now.'

'Why do you say "if"?' Caroline enquired.

Bernard grinned. 'That's lawyer's caution. We don't like making definite statements. I'm just observing that there is a black side, if one cares to look for it. I am all for the drug traffickers as our culprits. After all, they are already murderers, if only indirectly. The last thing we want is for the police to start looking elsewhere, because that could mean they were after one of us.'

Lottie listened to what Commissaire Orloff had to say. She sat ramrod still, her face closed and hostile. Orloff wondered if she might be about to attack him. But the anger was not directed at him.

'The worst mistake of my life,' she said bitterly, 'was to allow myself to be taken to a dinner-party in London towards the end of the war. Léon was there. He was a colonel then, and had just returned from some hideously dangerous mission. I was up from the country, where I'd been leading a dreary life running the family estate with nothing but a gang of land-girls. A stray German aeroplane, which had lost its way, had unloaded its bombs onto us. The house was blown to smithereens, our vegetables for which I had ploughed up the lawns were showered over half the village, and all we had worked for was gone. So I fled to Town to a friend. It was the time when London was being hit by rockets, but I didn't care. If Adolph Hitler had been going to kill me, he would have done it when the house went. And I fell flat on my face for Léon de Saint Brieuc, the great mysterious hero. More fool me!'

'Madame,' said Orloff, fascinated, but aiming to bring his witness to the point.

Lottie swept on: 'And what has that brought me? Nothing but misery. All these years battling with Léon, first over Estelle and then over Marie-France. And him mooning over his lost Josephine every blessed day of his life. I should have had that grotto pulled down long ago. But I suppose whoever it was would have found some other way of killing Marie-France. And now this! Are you really asking me to believe that my girls have been killed for their inheritance?'

'I would be failing in my duty, Madame, if I neglected this matter,' said Orloff, taking refuge in formality.

It seemed to steady her. 'What do you want to know?'

'Just this: who will now inherit your money? Do you have the disposal of it?'

Lottie shook her head. 'I do not. My father disapproved of my marriage, on principle, because Léon was not English. He disliked all foreigners. He refused to rebuild the house. Sold the whole estate. There is a new town built on it now. He tied up the money – and that which my grandmother was proposing to leave to me – so that if I had no direct heirs, it would not be swallowed up by the French family. Every penny will go to my nephew, Henry Bracebridge, and after him to his daughter, Caroline.'

'The Caroline Bracebridge who is here now?'

Lottie looked him straight in the eye. 'Yes. But please do not ask me to believe that a Bracebridge could be responsible for these dastardly crimes.'

Brigadier Kergrist met Commissaire Orloff at the kitchen door of Keralic.

'I have the report on the grotto, Commissaire,' he announced. 'I thought you might prefer to go through it on-site.'

Orloff looked pleased. 'Good of you, Brigadier,' he said. 'Let us walk down there. And I must bring you up to date on my interviews with the General and his wife. I think you will find it interesting.'

The grotto, once the haunt of lovers, was a forlorn wreck.

The iron grille had gone, removed for laboratory examination. Inside, all mystery had vanished and, in the pitiless light of day streaming in through the shattered roof, the shell mermaids on the walls looked down on a litter of dust and shards of mortar, ground into the patterned pebble floor.

Kergrist handed the laboratory report to Orloff. 'According to that,' he said, looking up at the sky, 'the vault became unsafe originally through water damage. There was a flat roof on top of it, and although there was a downpipe for drainage, the whole thing hadn't been cleaned for years. There was all sorts of debris up there – still is, in the corners. I've seen it. Rotting leaves and moss, mainly. That collected the water and held it, then, when a crack appeared in the roof, water began to get in. Part of the vault fell in last winter, after a storm. The damage was repaired by a local handyman, but the water started seeping through again. Our operator speeded up the work of the water. There was a round hole a metre wide in the top of the vault to let in light—'

'An oculus,' said Orloff.

'How much? Can't say I've ever heard the word. Anyway, the mortar of the stones round that hole, for half a metre, had been chipped loose. Then a large nail was hammered in between two stones and the rope attached to that. The murderer relied on one good tug of the rope to dislodge those two stones, and the shock would be enough to bring down the rest.'

'Which is exactly what happened,' murmured Orloff, scanning the report. 'Now, how was it done?'

'Probably from the top for the most part. It is not difficult to climb onto the roof. The bank the grotto is built into is almost to roof level. The insertion of the nail would have to be done from inside.'

Orloff frowned, examining a sketch in the report. 'It must have been quite high. No one could reach. Are we expected to believe that the murderer trailed down the garden with a ladder and was not seen?'

Kergrist let out a short bark of laughter. 'Our operator had everything laid on for him. The gardener, François, says he brought a step-ladder here the day after the Colonel arrived. The General wanted his opinion about the condition of the

144

roof, but it seems that the old gentleman never got round to doing it. The thing must be here still, under a heap of snow.'

'Let's find it,' said Orloff, striding out onto the paved apron between the grotto and the twin pools in front of it.

'I could get the men to do it,' Kergrist offered, eyeing Orloff's elegant shoes.

'It can't be far off,' said Orloff, kicking at a heap of snow drifted against the side wall.

He was rewarded immediately, as his foot struck metal. He began scraping away the snow to reveal the bottom end of a step-ladder. Kergrist grabbed the lowest step and slowly drew the ladder from the piled snow.

'I'll get it printed, but I would be surprised to find anything, Commissaire. Our man is too careful.'

Orloff wandered back into the grotto. Kergrist followed.

'So we know how it was done,' said the Commissaire, thoughtfully, looking up at the gaping hole where the vault used to be, 'but there is no hint of who did it.' He consulted the report. 'The work would take quite a time. At least a couple of hours and very likely more. But no particular strength.'

'Any one of them could have done it,' said Kergrist, grimly.

Orloff was re-reading a page of the report.

'There's a note here that I find interesting. You saw it?'

'From the architect they called in? Yes, I read it. That chap said there could be no means of telling whether or not the roof would collapse. I suppose he knows what he is talking about. If he's right, it seems a very chancy method of murdering someone.'

'Any fingerprints?'

'Not a thing. The surface of the stones is too rough to yield prints. And that nail is a whole lot cleaner than nails usually are, so that must have been wiped. The gate is not much use in that direction, either. You can't lift a print off a rope, and while there are dozens of prints round the lock there is nothing near where the rope was tied.' Kergrist frowned. 'That rope bothers me. If it hadn't been left there, who'd have suspected murder, with the state of that roof?'

'To me it suggests two possibilities,' said the Commissaire. 'One: that the murderer intended to be the first on the scene

145

and so remove the rope before anyone saw it. Or two: that the murderer could afford to leave it there.'

'What's that?'

'I am talking about someone to whom it was important that Marie-France's death should be recognised as murder immediately. The killing of the girl is linked with that of her mother. So someone who would not be suspected of the first crime would be very happy to leave that rope dangling from the grille.'

Kergrist stared. He had to admit that Orloff was good. He wondered how long it would have taken him to work that out.

'Who?' he asked.

'An invisible man,' said Orloff. 'There is no better cloak for a murderer than invisibility. And we have three invisible men for the murder of Estelle de Saint Brieuc.'

'Three!'

'The heirs of Keralic: Charles and Bernard de Montigny. And the heir to the cash: Henry Bracebridge.'

'We'll have to check on them. I'll get onto it right away.'

Orloff held up his hand. 'No need, Brigadier. I have had my eye on them from the start. It was fairly obvious that the de Montignys had an interest in this place and I persuaded an acquaintance in Scotland Yard to take a look at the Bracebridges for me. On that side, there is only the nephew, Henry, whom we now know to be Madame de Saint Brieuc's heir. We can forget him. He is safely stuck in his house in Suffolk with a well-attested broken ankle.'

'And the others?'

'Charles de Montigny can be ruled out, for doing the job personally, I mean. He has an alibi that stands up. He, too, is ill, in a clinic with a malady that comes through looking through the bottom of a glass.'

'What about the son?'

Orloff smiled. 'This is where it becomes interesting. On the night that Estelle was killed, Bernard de Montigny was no further away from here than Morlaix, a matter of about fifty kilometres.'

Léon was scrabbling among the notebooks and papers on the table in the study, muttering to himself. It really was too

146

irritating when things were not put back in their proper places.

He heard the door open.

'Caroline! What did you do with the Dien Bien Phu notes? That volume of the diary is missing, too. I'm sorry to go on about this, but you aren't very tidy and things are so easily lost.'

He looked round, surprised that she was not hurrying to the table to join in the search.

He was even more surprised to see Commissaire Orloff in the doorway.

'Oh, I beg your pardon, Commissaire. I thought you were my young niece. Such a nice child, but with a highly idiosyncratic way of arranging papers. What can I do for you?'

'I would like to use this room for an interrogation, General. The library is hardly adequate. People may need to pass through. It may take some little time.'

'That sounds very serious, Commissaire.'

'It is, General. I would also be obliged if the rest of the household could be kept away from this part of the house.'

Léon laid down the papers in his hand. 'Certainly, Commissaire. The room is yours. May I ask whom you are about to interrogate?'

Orloff gazed at him with a certain compassion. 'Bernard de Montigny and Mademoiselle Bracebridge.'

All vestige of colour left the old man's face.

'Oh, no!' he murmured. Then he straightened himself, almost stood to attention and said, 'I'll bring them to you myself.'

Caroline was sitting on a small chair in Uncle Léon's bedroom. If she turned her head, she could look out of the window, across the garden to the sweep of unbroken whiteness on the other side of the valley and the stark trees of the wood. Miraculously, the grey clouds were breaking up, revealing a patch of clear blue sky. The first rays of sunshine struck silver fire from the snow. It was the earliest hint of spring.

But not for her.

She shivered, although the room was warm. At the door stood a gendarme, apparently at ease, but ready for instant action should she try to leap through the window in search of freedom.

It was monstrous to feel herself under restraint, like all the nightmares in the world rolled into one. But this was no dream.

What were they doing to Bernard?

It was no use pretending to herself that this was routine questioning, the taking of yet another statement. Incarceration with a guardian policeman gave the lie to that. And she had had a glimpse of the faces of Brigadier Kergrist and the Commissaire before the study door had closed on Bernard.

She discovered that she was mortally afraid of Orloff.

Bernard said, 'You can't prove any of this, Commissaire.'

'You would be surprised what we can prove when we try,' Orloff replied. 'Please do not pretend that you did not know you were an heir to Keralic.'

'If you are talking about *partage*, yes, of course, I knew I would inherit something. But not the estate itself. My share would have been a piece of furniture or a picture.'

'And how did you feel about that?'

'About what?'

'The finish of the Saint Brieuc name. Your father's line come to an end because there were only daughters. And you having to stand back and watch it. You, who but for the stubbornness of Madame de Saint Brieuc would have been born a Saint Brieuc. One could understand that you could consider that you were robbed of your rights.'

Bernard reflected bitterly that the Commissaire had got his money's worth out of that dinner. He must have turned Josephine inside out.

Not that it made it any the less irregular. He had never heard of a police officer taking a witness out to dinner. He toyed with the idea that the indiscretion might be used as a handle – at dire need. And rejected the thought at once. It would be a rash man who tried conclusions with Maximilien Orloff.

'Until after Estelle's funeral, Commissaire, I did not know

148

the truth about my parentage. The man I had been brought up to believe was my father would never speak of my mother, whom he divorced when I was six years old. I have taken the habit of visiting her over the past few years, but she told me nothing.'

Orloff raised his eyebrows. 'Come, Monsieur, in your capacity as family lawyer, you must have come here from time to time. Is that not so?'

'Yes. What of it?'

'Then you must have observed that portrait of the General in the dining room. The resemblance is remarkable.'

'These things occur in families. He was my uncle, as far as I knew.'

'Monsieur, every member of the family seems to have known the truth, even a youngster like Marie-France, yet you persist in your claim that you yourself were in ignorance.'

'Strange as it may seem, Commissaire,' said Bernard, stiffly holding himself in check – losing his temper would suit Orloff's book, 'that is the truth.'

'Didn't you ever wonder?'

Bernard felt the trap closing round him. It was impossible to deny the charge, not when he had plagued his mother to tell him.

'Yes, I wondered from time to time.'

Orloff pounced on the admission, as Bernard knew he would.

'I suggest to you, Monsieur, that you did a great deal more than wonder. From what I have learnt of Estelle de Saint Brieuc, she would have taken particular pleasure in telling you.'

He paused, as if inviting Bernard to make a further damaging statement. None came from the tight-lipped young man.

'I also suggest that you decided to help yourself to what you considered as your rightful inheritance by removing first Estelle de Saint Brieuc and then her daughter.'

'But I wasn't here when Estelle was murdered!' Bernard pointed out.

'No, Monsieur. That was the heart of your plan. Because you were not, apparently, on-site for the first murder, no one

149

would suspect you of being the perpetrator of the second. Yet what we know about Estelle's movements on the night of her death suggests that she was keeping an appointment, outside the house but not far from it. Such a rendezvous would hardly be with someone already staying at Keralic, since it would be ridiculous to go out on a cold winter's night when one might meet comfortably indoors. Therefore, she was meeting someone from outside. Not, as we have now established, desperate drug pedlars. It was unlikely to be anyone from the town, and Georges Quennec was in Tokyo. But she was very likely to be meeting someone she knew well, a cousin, no less, who happened to be spending the night no further away than Morlaix.'

Bernard stared at the Commissaire. 'That is all supposition. Let me tell you that, much as I admire Keralic, I am in no position to maintain it. Neither is my father. Once the General has gone, we shall be obliged either to sell or to let it. I don't think that fits in with the motives you attribute to me.'

'Give me the credit for a little intelligence, Monsieur!' Orloff snapped. 'The estate is not the only inheritance of those murdered women. The Bracebridge fortune is more than enough to maintain Keralic.'

'Madame de Saint Brieuc would hardly leave that to me!'

'No. It has to return to her own family, to her nephew Henry and ultimately to his daughter, Caroline Bracebridge.'

Bernard's face whitened. 'Leave Caroline out of this!'

'Unfortunately, Monsieur, that is impossible. As yet, I have not decided if she is your accomplice or your dupe. I am about to find out,' said Orloff and turned to Kergrist. 'Brigadier, would you be so good as to fetch Mademoiselle Bracebridge?'

Kergrist went without a word. He knew enough of Orloff now to recognise that bland tone. Whatever was the man up to?

As soon as he had gone, Orloff rose.

'That will be all for the moment, Monsieur de Montigny. Please hold yourself in readiness for further questioning.'

Bernard jumped up. 'I intend to call a lawyer.'

'That may well be wise,' Orloff agreed.

Bernard marched to the door, vaguely surprised to hear the Commissaire following him. He flung it open, and there, in the corridor, was Caroline, with Brigadier Kergrist.

She flew to him. 'Bernard! Bernard! What's going on?'

His arms closed round her. 'It's all right, my darling. I won't let them harm you.'

Kergrist made a move to separate them, but was stopped by a faint shake of Orloff's head.

Caroline appeared to be entirely satisfied with her lover's impossible promise. She leant against him, thankful for his nearness.

'I don't understand,' she murmured.

'They can't prove anything against me, because there is nothing to prove,' he assured her. 'Even if on the night that Estelle was killed I did happen to be at Morlaix—'

Caroline sprang away from him, as if the physical contact had burnt her.

'Morlaix! Oh, no! I don't believe it!'

'Believe what?'

'That woman! You're still seeing her!'

'Good God, Caroline, are you still on about that nonsense?' Bernard shouted. 'Don't you trust me at all?'

'Estelle—'

'You'd believe her rather than me? Don't—'

Orloff stepped between them. 'What about Estelle?' he enquired.

'Nothing!' replied Bernard, shortly.

'You call it nothing?' shrieked Caroline. She turned to the Commissaire. 'Do you want to know what he was doing in Morlaix? I can tell you. He was visiting his mistress. Rosalie Beguy.'

Bernard grabbed her by the shoulders and shook her. 'Caro! Stop it! Madame Beguy is a client.'

'Ha!' Caroline snorted, struggling to free herself.

'She is also eighty-five.'

The fight went out of her. 'Eighty-five!'

'That's right.'

'Estelle said you were lovers!'

'Monsieur de Montigny might conceivably have an alibi if they were,' Orloff put in.

Caroline cast him a wild glance. 'Estelle must have been off her head!'

'Not she!' said Bernard, grimly. 'She spun you a tale last

year for the purpose of breaking up our relationship. To spite me.'

Over his shoulder, Caroline glimpsed a sudden interest in Brigadier Kergrist's face.

'Don't say another word, Bernard! It's all my fault. I've been so stupid.'

'I doubt if it is news to the Commissaire that Estelle and I did not have much to say to each other,' he replied, wearily. 'So let's set the record straight. Madame Beguy is a most valuable client. Her main amusement is changing her Will to annoy her rapacious family, who are longing for her to die. She is too old to travel to Paris, so I go to her in Morlaix every time she wishes to make a change – and very profitable it is too, for me.'

Caroline looked at him wonderingly. 'Why didn't you tell me last year?'

'Did you give me a chance? And, my love, I confess I was acting the goat. All I was looking for was an excuse to persuade myself that I was not in love with you. You were not at all the sort of girl I had intended to marry.'

'Thanks very much,' she said, but without rancour.

'I thought I should have a rich, well-connected French wife, who could advance my career. It wasn't until I had lost you that I discovered that no one else would do. For months now I have been trying to think of a way of getting you back.'

'Oh, Bernard!' said Caroline and flung herself into his arms.

'Very interesting,' said Commissaire Orloff, effectively breaking up the reconciliation. 'I have changed my mind. I think I will postpone my further interrogation of Mademoiselle Bracebridge. Come along, Brigadier. I want to go back to Tremerrec.'

Kergrist followed him along the corridor, under the disapproving painted eyes of Saint Brieuc ancestors in gilt frames. He wondered if Orloff had achieved his objective. That confrontation was no coincidence, but carefully engineered by the Commissaire. There was no knowing what he would do next. The man was as full of tricks as a bag of monkeys. And most of them were clean against accepted police procedure. All the morning, Kergrist had been asking himself how a mere Brigadier could tell a Commissaire that he should not take out to dinner a woman who was certainly a witness and might become a suspect.

At two o'clock, in the bar down on the quay, Paul Pleubian called to his wife to mind the counter, put on his cap and his muffler, and started up the hill towards the cathedral. Soon, he took off the scarf as a welcome warmish breeze blew through the windy town. The sky was clear and lying snow was beginning to slide down roofs and melt away from bushes. Underfoot, it was still hard-packed and slippery, crunching under his boots.

He turned into the deserted Place. One or two shops were opening their doors, but the customers were not yet venturing out, the going being dangerous, especially for the elderly. The Commune was coming in for much criticism for dragging its feet over clearing the snow.

At the butcher's shop, Odile Quennec was putting on her apron, while her husband could be seen, through the open door of the cold-room, taking down barded and tied roasting beef.

'Madame, Monsieur,' said Paul, glad that there were no early customers. 'I thought I should come.'

The welcoming smile faded from Madame Quennec's face.

'Georges?' she said faintly.

Her husband emerged from the cold-room. He was a heavily built man, with a dangerously high colour. All at once, he seemed to find difficulty in breathing.

'What's up?' he gasped.

Paul looked uncomfortably from one to the other. 'He's been at my place for a couple of hours, drinking a lot more than he usually does. Talking very wild, too. Saying he's going to get even with the Saint Brieucs.'

'Where is he now?' Odile demanded.

'I don't know, Madame. He went off about half an hour ago. I was worried about him.'

She glanced at her husband, who nodded. Then she began to untie her apron-strings.

'It's very good of you to take such trouble, Monsieur,' she said, hanging the clean white cotton on a hook near the till.

153

'My poor Georges needs his friends. Thank you for coming.'

'He may just have gone home,' said Paul doubtfully.

'I'll go down there and see.'

'But if he isn't there, Madame?'

'Then I will go to Keralic.'

'Where have you been?' Lottie demanded, shooting a malevolent glance at Caroline and Bernard as they entered the drawing room, where they found the others drinking coffee.

'We went out to lunch,' said Bernard. 'I told Berthe not to lay for us.'

'Good of you!' snapped Lottie, unappeased.

'We went to the Crêperie in the village,' said Caroline, hoping to introduce a note of normal conversation. 'It was quite good.'

The effort fell flat.

'Ashamed to show your faces at the lunch table, were you?' Lottie enquired, ignoring her.

'We wanted to be alone,' Bernard told her, in a calm voice. 'We're getting married very soon.'

'You can't do that in gaol,' Lottie pointed out.

Colonel Clermont cleared his throat in an embarrassed manner and muttered something inaudible.

Josephine fired up. 'Whatever you may think, Madame, I, for one, do not believe my son capable of murder!'

'You hardly know him,' Lottie retorted crushingly. 'How can you tell what he would do?'

'That is quite enough, my dear,' said Léon, suddenly asserting himself. 'We are all of us liable to be questioned time and again. That does not mean that we are necessarily guilty.'

'It's all right,' said Bernard. 'I don't mind what she says. She'll have to take it all back, later on!'

To the general astonishment, Caroline burst into tears.

'How can you go on like this?' she sobbed. 'Don't any of you have hearts? I know it's awful for Aunt Lottie and Uncle Léon because they have lost Estelle and Marie-France, but what about us? That horrible man is trying to pin it on Bernard and ruin both our lives, just when we should be starting to be happy together.'

Bernard gathered her into his arms.

154

'Oh, my dear child!' said Lottie, non-plussed for once in her life.

Commissaire Orloff returned to his office after lunch to find a package on his desk. It contained Estelle's red woollen dress and the laboratory report on the stain on the bodice.

Orloff read it through, examining the dress for himself. Then he picked up the phone to ask the Brigadier to come along.

Kergrist came quickly. 'Ah, the dress!' he said, eagerly. 'What do they say about it?'

Orloff tossed him the report. 'See for yourself!'

The Brigadier read the laboratory findings.

Twice.

'I don't believe it!' he said.

'We have to. The analysis is exactly the same as the other samples they were given. There can't be any mistake, Brigadier. The stain on that dress was made by the water of the lake at Keralic.'

CHAPTER 9

'I told you,' said Orloff. 'One little detail in a hundred pays off.'

Kergrist stared. 'You were expecting this?'

'I don't know what I was expecting. All I started from was the point that Estelle had, apparently, changed her dress. I wondered why.'

'The cold night,' said Kergrist.

'Yes. But surely the fur coat would have been enough to keep her warm. So I wanted to look at the dress. And I found it torn and stained.'

Kergrist picked up the dress and examined it. 'I can't think, offhand, of any way that stain could have been made.'

'The first thing we must establish is if that dress was stained when Estelle wore it at dinner on the evening of her death.'

'It looks rather new. No signs of wear at all.'

'Whom do you think would be most likely to have noticed?'

'Madame de Montigny is the best dressed,' said Kergrist, with a sidelong glance at the Commissaire.

'No, she won't do. I know! Mademoiselle Bracebridge. Now, I want her brought in, which will give her a fright but won't hurt her. And since young de Montigny will certainly come hot-foot after her, we might as well fetch them both. Will you arrange that?'

'Right away,' said Kergrist and dashed out.

He was back very quickly, to find Orloff gazing thoughtfully at the dress.

'We should have them in twenty minutes at the outside.'

'Good. I must have the answer to that question before I indulge in any flights of fancy.'

The Brigadier felt the old surge of resentment again, but

156

this time there was a difference: it was against himself, for not having noticed the stain on the dress when it was actually in his hands during the search of Estelle's room, and for not understanding its significance.

'That dress is important, isn't it?' he said.

Orloff nodded. 'In my opinion, the whole case may turn on it.'

Kergrist hesitated. It was a moment of decision: of whether or not to accept the methods of this strange man, most of which cut right across all his training; or of succumbing to the insidious charm of Maximilien Orloff.

He drew a deep breath and took the plunge. 'I would be glad to hear your "flights of fancy", Commissaire.'

Orloff smiled, aware that he had beguiled yet another sound policeman into stepping out of the rut of routine. Kergrist was not the first, nor would he be the last.

'Would you really? Without waiting for Mademoiselle Bracebridge to tell us if the dress was stained?'

'Estelle de Saint Brieuc would not have worn it with a stain on it.'

'That is my reading of her character, too, Brigadier. Very well, let us start with that dress. We know what the stain is: water of the lake at Keralic, which has a wide variety of all sorts of things in it so as to make it unique. The problem is how that stain got there.'

'She wasn't wearing it when she went into the lake.'

'Indeed she wasn't. The stain is only over part of the bodice.' With one long forefinger, Orloff traced the water-mark on the bright wool. 'Also the shoulders and the top of one arm. There can be no possible reason for anyone to take this dress and dip it into the lake. Rule that out and there is only one explanation left.'

'Oh?' Kergrist muttered, unwilling to admit that he could not see what it was.

'Estelle was not wearing this dress when she went into the lake, as you so rightly pointed out, but she *was* wearing it when she was killed.'

The Brigadier sat up. 'She drowned in the lake.'

Orloff shook his head. 'That is the inference we were supposed to draw. The indisputable fact is that she drowned

157

in lake water. Just as the dress was stained with it. The only way to reconcile those two facts is by imagining a receptacle filled with water drawn from the lake, something just big enough to take her head and shoulders, when held down by a firm hand on the back of the neck.'

'There was a bruise!'

'Others, too, which looked random to the pathologist, but which could have been caused by her struggle to free herself. She would kick, for a short time. Death by drowning in fresh water is much quicker than in the sea. A matter of about four or five minutes. Brigadier, we need another examination of that body.'

'An exhumation?'

'What sort of grave is it?'

'The family vault.'

'That makes it a whole lot simpler. I must see that body tonight.'

'It's rather short notice,' said Kergrist, diffidently. 'There may be difficulties.'

'I think I possess enough clout to take a few short cuts,' Orloff replied, unconcerned. 'And I want the lid kept on this, please. I don't want word filtering through to Keralic.'

'Our operator has to be one of them,' Kergrist pointed out. 'If Estelle was killed when she was wearing that dress without a coat over it, it must have been in the house.'

'Very likely,' said Orloff.

'The pathologist didn't suggest that the body had been moved after death, Commissaire.'

'All that means is that our operator moved very quickly. While the blood was still fluid, in fact. Post-mortem staining does not set in immediately. There is an interval of perhaps half an hour, or even more. Time enough for the murderer to change the dress and transport the body to the lake where it could be found with no tell-tale marks inconsistent with death by drowning in it. And, remember, the body was immersed for around twelve hours. She was not in the water long enough for any big changes to take place, but saturation was bound to confuse the issue a bit.'

Kergrist rubbed his hand over his chin, thoughtfully.

'There is a lot I don't understand yet. If you are right,

Commissaire, and I think you must be, the murderer dressed the body up – skirt, jumper, fur coat, gloves – to create the impression that she had gone to the lake under her own steam.'

'So it would appear. Elaborate, but clever.'

'But why go to the trouble of taking off the dress? The heavy coat would have been enough on its own.'

'My guess,' said Orloff, 'is that the tear in the dress was the problem. It must have happened during the struggle. And there would be no way of accounting for it. It would be unlikely for the dress under a coat to be torn in the course of a suicide or an accident. It suggests violence, straightaway. Our operator is a most meticulous person. He – or she – would see at once that it was too great a risk to leave the dress on the body, and was resourceful enough to make an instant decision about what to do with it. We even have a witness.'

Kergrist jumped. 'We have?'

'Madame de Saint Brieuc. She said she heard her daughter go downstairs, then come back up again, but only for a few minutes before going down again. She didn't, of course. She was talking about the sound of the bedroom door, which she recognised. What she actually heard was that door being opened or shut, once by Estelle, twice by her murderer, fetching the clothes.'

The Brigadier considered the matter. 'Wasn't it even more risky to put the dress in the wardrobe?' he objected.

The Commissaire shook his head. 'Far from it, if you think about it. What was our operator to do with it? It could not be simply missing, in case someone thought to look for it. In any case, it would be difficult to dispose of. Suppose it had been hidden, and we had turned it up in the course of a routine search? Immediately, suspicions would have been aroused.'

'The murderer could have taken it away.'

'Not if he – or she – was living in the house, and would not care to be observed leaving with a parcel. No, Brigadier, the wardrobe was the only suitable place.'

'Where it might slip through police scrutiny,' said Kergrist bitterly. 'As it did. I had it in my hands and I didn't give it a second thought.'

Why, he tormented himself, did Orloff have the imagination to follow up on the dress when I did not?

'Put that behind you, Brigadier,' Orloff advised. 'I went after the dress only because it was a small jarring detail. Madame de Saint Brieuc is not the sort of woman to tolerate a jumper and skirt at the dinner-table. It doesn't matter who unearthed the dress. The important point is that we have it and it has turned the case upside down.'

'I expect you know more about the habits of these people than I do,' said Kergrist, humbly.

'Maybe so. In which case, stop blaming yourself. From what I have seen of you, you are a good detective and you will have learnt from this. Perhaps in future my method over details will come in useful. I don't advise that you copy some of the other things I do,' he added, with that smile. 'I have my own ways of doing things and have built up a reputation of being highly original. Ah, I can see by your face that a report has reached you of my presence in Lazardrieux last night. Highly unethical, but you would be amazed at what I learn from such things. It may comfort you to know that there are mandarins in the Ministry of the Interior who are longing for me to make a bad mistake and fall flat on my face, so that they may have the pleasure of chopping off my head.'

'I hope they never get the chance,' said Kergrist and meant it.

Orloff laughed. 'I try to keep the results rolling in. So let us return to my reasoning, which can be shattered in a moment if Mademoiselle Bracebridge says she saw the stain on the dress that evening.'

'Which is exactly what one might expect a murderer to say,' Kergrist pointed out.

'Fancy her, do you? She is strong enough. But leave aside the question of *who* for the moment. Let us go on working on *how*. And, more importantly, *where*. Shortly, we will go to Keralic and see if we can find where Estelle was killed.'

'There must be a lot of bathrooms in that place. I don't see how there will be any traces left now,' said Kergrist, gloomily.

'Somehow, I don't fancy a bathroom,' said the Commissaire. 'In my experience, bathplugs always leak slightly and we don't know how long it took to fill up the lethal receptacle.

160

The water from the lake must have been brought up bucket by bucket, probably at night when everyone else had gone to bed, except Marie-France, who was usually out and in the habit of coming home late. The door would be left unlocked for her, so there would be no problem there, except the risk of coming face to face with her with a bucket of dirty water in one's hand. That would take a bit of explaining.'

'There are plenty of doors,' Kergrist pointed out. 'All those long windows open. Marie-France would use the kitchen door to come in.'

'So she would. The next point to consider is how the dead body of Estelle was transported from the house to the lake. I doubt if anyone could carry her that far, and her clothes did not show signs of considerable dragging. So there must have been some form of transport. A car would not pass down that path and a tractor would make a noise.'

'A wheelbarrow,' Kergrist suggested.

'Yes,' Orloff agreed. 'One that has been well oiled so that it does not squeak.'

'If we are lucky, we might find one with a little tuft of fur caught in somewhere. We never did find a bit to match the piece missing from the sleeve of Estelle's coat.'

'Bravo, Brigadier! And there's something else we can look for.'

'What?'

'Some muddied planks. That wheelbarrow, or whatever it was, must have been tricky to manage. It tipped over when it was being manoeuvred onto the grass to get to the lake, and the body fell into that rhododendron – how else explain that fall? It would be even more awkward to wheel it across a stretch of sodden grass. Remember those straight lines in the muddy tracks there? I thought they might have been made by the boat they used to fish her out. They could just as well have been made by planks forming a causeway for a laden barrow.'

There was a knock at the door and a gendarme came in to announce the arrival of Caroline and Bernard.

Orloff sprang up. 'Here we go!' he said cheerfully. 'My theory may be demolished by one word from that young woman.'

Kergrist muttered something inaudible, but which boded

no good for the witness.

Caroline's eyes opened wide with amazement at the question.

'Stain?' she repeated. 'On that red dress? I should think not. That was the first time Estelle wore it. It was brand-new. What stain?'

But Commissaire Orloff was in the business of asking questions, not answering them.

Georges Quennec was in a ditch. He had little recollection of how he came to be there. Only a vague memory of a long session in Paul's bar and then walking along the quay. He shook his head to clear it, and remembered crossing the bridge.

Shaking his head was a painful process, and not only because too much drink made it feel as though it belonged to someone else. There was another, more local, pain. Gingerly, he put up a hand to feel. He found a sticky lump. His fingers felt sticky, too. He pulled them down to eye-level and saw that they were covered in blood.

Something wet plopped onto the end of his nose. He put up a finger to explore.

Water.

He looked up and received a second dose in the eye. Above him, glistening droplets lined the bare branches of a tree, as the snow melted in the new-found warmth of the sun. Beyond the tree, the sky took on a deeper blue.

It came to him that he was very wet. There was snow all round him, piled up in a drift, soft crystalline whiteness that would very soon turn to water. Already there was a steady trickle running down the middle of the road, as the thaw spread.

A figure came round a bend, plodding steadily up the incline. Georges watched the trim familiar shape approach. In his fuddled state it was no special surprise that his mother should be there.

Odile came to an abrupt halt when she spotted a person in the ditch, then came sliding over the melting snow.

'Georges! What are you doing there?'

He smiled foolishly. 'I fell over, I think. I've cut my head.'

She bent down to pull him out. For a small woman, she was surprisingly strong.

'You're coming home with me,' she said sternly, as he clung to her to keep his balance.

'No, Mother, I remember now. I have to go to Keralic.'

'Not in that state you won't. You're drunk and bleeding. You're coming home now. And I mean home. Not that studio.'

'Yes, Mother,' said Georges, and fainted.

Commissaire Orloff, Brigadier Kergrist and a small group of men were standing by the muddy trodden grass between the path and the lake. The sudden warmth had melted away all traces of ice. On the lake, water fowl were peeping out from their home in the reeds round the island. The camellia buds were showing bright pink in the sun.

'See those straight lines?' said Orloff to one of the men. 'I want casts of those, please. And samples of the mud. There is a bit of decent light to work in at the moment, but it won't last. Everything must be done before dark.' He turned round and surveyed the scene. 'Now, is there anything we might have missed? I think we should have a lot of close-ups of that rhododendron. The body must have crashed against it with some force. A pattern of broken twigs might reconstruct the fall for us. Look! There! And there!'

Kergrist followed his pointing finger. 'Yes,' he said eagerly. 'Over here, too, Commissaire.'

The photographer started work.

Orloff walked over the grass, keeping well clear of the tracks where the men were already preparing the casts. He halted at the water's edge.

'It's not very deep just here,' he remarked, peering down. 'If she was tipped in over there ...' He turned to Kergrist. 'I wonder if she fell neatly or if she stuck. Our operator would need to have her further out, if she was to sink, which I suppose was his intention. It must have been a nasty shock when she was found so quickly. She would have popped up again soon enough – drowned bodies do – but by that time a good deal of the evidence would have been destroyed. These tracks, for instance.'

'The family here did their best to obliterate them,' said Kergrist. 'One – or two – of them must have been keen on that. They did a good job.'

'But not quite good enough, fortunately. Have we the photographs handy?'

Kergrist opened the briefcase from which he was rarely parted. 'Here, Commissaire.'

Together they re-examined the prints.

'Wait a minute,' said the Brigadier, suddenly. 'Let me have a look at that one again.'

He all but snatched it from Orloff's hand, stared at it for a moment, then raised his head.

'I thought there was something different,' he said, thrusting the photograph back into the Commissaire's hand.

He strode over to a large camellia bush. He tussled with it for a moment, then emerged with a stout length of timber. It was a branch from some tree, forked at one end, trimmed roughly to make a prop. Behind him, the camellia, robbed of its crutch, sagged sideways.

'How about this, Commissaire?' said Kergrist, brandishing his trophy. 'Just right for pushing the body out into the middle of the lake?'

Orloff looked from the photographs to the broken bush and saw that it had been that way on the morning that Estelle was taken out of the water.

'One of your little details, eh?' said Kergrist, with a sly grin. He took a closer look at the branch. 'Hey! What's this?'

Orloff peered at the branch. A few dark hairs were caught in a piece of broken bark.

'The fur coat?' Kergrist suggested.

'It looks like it. Congratulations, Brigadier.' Orloff considered the find. 'That forked end. That would hook round the jaw. I wonder if it made that bruise?'

'Could be!' Kergrist handed the branch carefully to one of his men.

'Sir, I remember that branch,' said the gendarme. 'It was lying on the grass, over there, when we arrived, after they had pulled her out of the lake.'

The Brigadier looked pleased. After all, it was his find. 'I doubt if that will prove a good subject for finger-prints,' he remarked, with a trace of bitterness.

'You can't win them all,' said Orloff. 'Let's see what they've found up at the house.'

He set off briskly up the path. The earliest flowers of spring were peeping through the disappearing snow, but the Commissaire had no eyes for them.

A young gendarme, his eyes bright with excitement, met them as they entered the courtyard.

'We've got them, Commissaire. A barrow and some planks.'

'Good work. Load them into the van. Then come to the house. We must start work inside.'

The man rushed off, while Orloff and Kergrist went to the kitchen door.

'You again!' Berthe exclaimed. 'What have you done with my Antoine?'

'He is under lock and key until the *juge d'instruction* has seen him,' Kergrist told her, and added, grimly, 'You might end up there yourself if you try any tricks.'

'Ha!' said Berthe, defiantly, but, having had one dose of the cells at the Gendarmerie and not anxious for another, she stepped back to let them in.

The General was waiting for them in the drawing room. He was alone.

'I understand that you wish to make a search of the entire house, Commissaire,' he said formally. 'You have my permission to do so. Also, neither my wife nor my guests have any objection to your searching their belongings.'

I wonder how he managed that, thought Orloff, who had envisaged an almighty tussle with Lottie, no matter what the actual laws on right of search might be. He made Léon a small bow, as befitting the old man's formality.

'Thank you, General. We shall be as quick as we can, and create as small a disturbance as possible.'

'My family and guests are assembled in the library. I will join them. Perhaps you would care to start in this room, then we may all move in here and leave the rest of the house free for you.'

It was not precisely Orloff's plan, but a General was still a

165

General, and the arrangements were intended to help.

'You are most co-operative, General. Thank you.'

'Not at all, Commissaire. It is my plain duty,' Léon replied, and with great dignity walked to the double doors to the library.

Orloff called him back.

'One thing more, General. There is a large camellia down by the lake. Part of it is broken off and propped up.'

A look of puzzlement crossed the old face.

'Very strange that, Commissaire. Someone moved that prop.'

'Do you know when?'

Léon shook his head. 'I didn't notice it until after the funeral, when I resumed my daily walk. I am a creature of habit, but while Estelle was unburied, I could not bring myself to go into the garden.'

'Who might have handled that prop?'

'François, my gardener,' replied the General promptly. 'Oh, yes, and Edouard, too. Colonel Clermont. He was with me when we saw it lying on the grass. He replaced it for me. Is it important?'

'Thank you, General,' said Orloff, not committing himself, and the old man passed into the library.

'Fat chance of prints on that branch,' Kergrist muttered as the door closed.

The gendarmes bunched in the kitchen doorway, waiting for orders.

'Right,' said Orloff. 'You all know what we are looking for. Get to it. If you find anything, report straight to the Brigadier, who will be with me.'

They left the men searching in the kitchen, dining room and drawing room. They passed through the library where all eyes followed them. Madame de Saint Brieuc, thought Kergrist, resembled a volcano ready to go off pop. He considered briefly his own dear wife and wondered what he would have done if she had grown into a virago. The General must be a man of infinite patience.

'The bedrooms?' he said, as they passed into the anteroom.

But Orloff was heading for the small door opposite the staircase.

166

The flower-room, thought Kergrist. Funny place to start.

He followed the Commissaire inside. It was cold and dank.

'For my money, this is the place,' said Orloff, unexpectedly. 'Look at that plastic bin under the bench. It is big enough to drown anyone held head down in it. Much better than any bathtub.'

He pulled out his handkerchief, draped it over his hand and gently drew the bin forward.

It was empty.

'There's a spot of water in the bottom, in that groove,' said Kergrist, peering in.

Orloff crawled under the bench. 'There's a bucket at the back. I wonder if that, too, might still be damp.'

The Brigadier gazed round. 'You are right, Commissaire. This place has everything. Privacy, for who is arranging flowers in the middle of winter, especially at night? And it has its own outer door.'

Carefully, he tried the rusty key in the lock. It turned easily and silently. He pulled at the door. That, too, moved soundlessly, the corroded hinges well and recently oiled.

'This gives onto the back of the house, Commissaire. There are no bedrooms on that side, only the top corridor. You could pass with buckets and wheelbarrows all night and no one would hear a thing.'

He turned back to the bin, examining it closely. 'Here! What's this?'

'Found something?' enquired Orloff from under the bench.

'There's a rough spot on the rim, and a thread caught in it.'

'From the dress?'

'Looks more like a nylon stocking.'

The Commissaire backed out from under the bench, to scrutinise the bin.

'That settles it. It was in here that Estelle's stockings were torn. Get the men in. I want this room gone over inch by inch, please. With a bit of luck that bin and bucket should reveal traces of lake water. It is simple enough to reconstruct what happened that night. Estelle had arranged to meet someone for a very private talk. What better place than the flower-room, with no one to overhear? And no risk of being seen coming out of someone else's bedroom. Just perfect for our operator, with that outside door.'

Kergrist looked at him curiously. 'You came straight here, Commissaire.'

'Thinking of all the rooms in this house, this one seemed to have the most possibilities.'

'Do you also know the identity of our operator?'

'I think so. But I don't want to stick my neck out yet, which no doubt will surprise you. On the face of it, anyone in this house could have set this up.'

'Or Bernard de Montigny with the assistance of someone inside. For carrying the buckets of lake water. I don't see how he had the time to do that, having come from Morlaix. Not even if he used the wheelbarrow to transport that bin and the bucket to fill it,' said Kergrist, regretfully. 'It would be very heavy, even if only half-full, which is the minimum depth he would need.'

'He's waiting for you at Tremerrec. You may have a good go at him and the girl when we are back.'

'I shall look forward to that, Commissaire. He thinks he's too clever by half, that one.'

'We are going to have to move quickly, Brigadier. Our man must know by now that we are closing in. I hope the laboratory will get moving tonight.'

'I alerted them. They've promised to work overtime.'

'I hope they'll keep at it all night. Or at least give us enough to go on. There is no proof yet. And tomorrow I want to wrap up this case.'

The cemetery was in the shadow of the cathedral, a neat and tidy place, after the Breton habit, of sombre memorials and gravel paths. The moon was up, reflecting dimly off polished granite, stones and crosses deceiving the eye, taking on strange shapes in the fitful gleams as clouds crossed the sky. Beyond the high Calvary which watched over the tranquil dead, the solid mass of Gothic building blocked out the lights of the town square, deserted at this late hour.

A small group of men stood clustered round the entrance to the Saint Brieuc vault, as, by the glare of torches, a shiny new coffin was hoisted out of the black gaping hole in the floor of the mortuary chapel.

168

Not a word was uttered, as if all were touched by a sense of sacrilege, of daring to pre-empt Doomsday by a raising of the dead.

Brigadier Kergrist shuffled his feet and wondered what the Commissaire hoped to gain by this macabre exercise. Why couldn't the man be content with the pathologist's report?

There was a trolley waiting, to wheel the coffin to the gravediggers' shed in the far corner. The undertaker's men loaded it, and they all trailed after it, Orloff, deep in conversation with the pathologist, bringing up the rear.

Lights blazed suddenly in the shed and the coffin was transferred to a trestle table erected in the centre. They crowded in, hampered by tools and discarded flower-urns, while the undertaker unscrewed the lid. A sweet waft of corruption filled the air. The youngest gendarme ran out, choking.

'Right, Commissaire,' said the pathologist, pulling on a pair of rubber gloves. 'What do you want to see first?'

He was a plump, middle-aged man, with an aura of jollity, which sat oddly on him, considering the nature of his trade. His secretary, a severe elderly lady who did not appear to be in the least affected either by the ambiance of the place or the nature of the grisly details about to be revealed, opened her notebook.

'The position of the bruises,' said Orloff. 'In the light of the new evidence, you understand. The one at the back of the neck. Could that have been made by the pressure of a hand?'

'Let's have a squint at it,' said the pathologist, lifting the corpse to a sitting position. 'Come up, my beauty!'

Another young policeman dashed out.

Orloff and the doctor peered at the bruise.

'Very possibly,' said the latter. 'And these bruises on the arms could have been caused either by the attacker's hands or by thrashing about when she was up-ended in the bin of water. There isn't a complete hand-print of bruises, but she wouldn't have been held that way. She would be seized by the tops of her arms and then her head pushed down into the water, maybe with the heel of the hand.'

Methodically, each bruise was examined, and a pattern emerged of a desperate attempt to hold onto life, and an inexorable progress towards the still waters of the lake.

Reluctantly, Kergrist admitted to himself that the Commissaire knew what he was doing: after this, there would be no way that a clever lawyer could raise doubts at a trial. A man hunted by Orloff was as good as lost from the start.

'The bruise on the jaw,' the Commissaire was saying; 'could that have been made by a branch?'

'Indeed it could. There are slight abrasions on the skin. Anything else, Commissaire?'

'We now know that the body was moved shortly after death—'

'If I had observed any indication of that I would have mentioned it in my initial report,' the doctor broke in, sharply.

'I am not suggesting that you were careless in any way,' said Orloff, 'but this is bound to be raised in court.'

'Yes, I see that,' said the doctor, mollified. 'Post-mortem staining is a strange thing. It does not occur immediately, although the body fluids are draining down to whatever position the corpse is in. Tight clothing affects it, and she was wearing a corset. There are no signs that the shoulders, hips or knees rested on a hard surface, but if she was moved immediately after death, while the blood was still fluid, it would not drain down into its final position until she was safely in the lake.'

'What sort of time interval are we talking about?'

The pathologist shrugged. 'Half an hour. An hour. Not long.'

'Long enough,' said Orloff, and signalled to the undertaker to close up the coffin.

Kergrist heard the Commissaire thanking the doctor. He was glad it was over. Only pride had kept him from following his men in fleeing from the stench. Through the open door of the shed, he could see their shadows, as they stood to one side, indulging in a quiet and much-needed smoke.

'She really didn't have a chance, Commissaire,' the pathologist was saying. 'Not once she was in that bin, head first. Nor did that poor kid of hers, when the grotto roof fell on her. I hope you catch the bastard.'

'Rest assured,' said Orloff. 'I will.'

170

CHAPTER 10

Morning brought a general thaw. Warm air blew over the land, drifted snow melted into streams, and sun poured in through the windows.

Josephine astonished the household by appearing in the dining room for breakfast. Berthe was surprised into putting down a hot coffee-pot on the polished table, which provoked a screech from Lottie. Caroline leapt up to lay a place for her future mother-in-law.

'Thank you, dear,' Josephine said, seating herself. 'I was so relieved last night when Bernard rang to say the police were letting you both go.'

'They'll be after me again this morning,' said Bernard, grimly. 'Thank God, Caro seems to be out of it now.'

'I wish I could be so sure,' she said doubtfully. 'Brigadier Kergrist went on at me for hours. I think he did believe me in the end. Aunt Lottie, is it true that I am in line for inheriting your money now?'

The old woman spread butter carefully on a slice of bread. 'Your father gets it first, and you after him. Unless that woman he's married starts producing a brood. Then you would have to share it.'

'Marcia? She'd have a fit. Besides, she's over forty.'

'And how old is Henry now? I forget.'

'Fifty,'

'Then you are in for a long wait, aren't you? How about that, Bernard?'

'I'm not marrying Caroline for her expectations, Aunt,' he replied, coolly. 'There is nothing to stop Henry spending it all, is there?'

Lottie shook her head.

171

'Well, then,' said Bernard. 'I only count on certainties. I should like to say, here and now, that I have not been murdering people so that eventually I could get my hands on Keralic. I hope you will take my word for that. I can't expect the police to believe my denials, but there is no way that they can prove something that didn't happen, and I am pinning my hopes on French justice.'

'Ho!' scoffed Lottie. 'Don't tell me no one is ever wrongly convicted in France. You, of all people, should know that, Bernard.'

He looked displeased. 'I need no reminding, Aunt. I was hoping that no one would raise the point, for the sake of my mother and my fiancée.'

'Bernard, I'm not a fool!' said Caroline, on the brink of tears. 'Of course I know the police can make mistakes. It's rather important that they don't, this time.'

As soon as the Commissaire arrived at the gendarmerie, Brigadier Kergrist marched into Orloff's office, his hands full of papers.

'The boys at the lab have turned up trumps,' he announced. 'I think they must have worked most of the night. They've phoned through all the results so far. The proper reports will follow.'

'Excellent,' said the Commissaire, who did not care a jot about official 'channels' and bypassed them whenever possible. 'Let me see what you have.'

Kergrist drew up a chair to the other side of the desk, and spread out the notes he had taken down over the telephone.

'First, the stuff from the flower-room. There are traces of algae and such from the lake in both the bin and the bucket. Plenty of fingerprints on both, but only old ones belonging to Madame de Saint Brieuc, Berthe Guegan and Estelle, all of whom used the place in the summer and up to Christmas. There are also smudges, superimposed on the prints. The lab interprets these as made by gloves.'

'Just what we might expect,' said Orloff. 'Go on.'

'The same sets of prints on the bench, shelves and vases.'

'All perfectly innocent. Maybe.'

'The thread that was caught in the rim of the bin is of nylon

172

and the type used in hosiery. It is an exact match to the tights Estelle was wearing.'

'I would have been surprised if it hadn't been. Go on.'

'The door yielded nothing. It is of roughish wood and the lock and key are both clean, which means that they have been wiped.'

'We know our operator is careful,' Orloff remarked, not visibly discouraged. 'The only thing I had hoped to establish was that Estelle was killed in the flower-room. So I am satisfied.'

Kergrist turned to another sheet of notes.

'The wheelbarrow: prints belonging to François the gardener, as might be expected. Some of them are smudged. Again, the lab says gloved hands. The small tuft of hairs caught between one handle and the body of the barrow are of the same type as Estelle's fur coat. That is also true of the bit on the branch that was holding up that bush,' he added, referring to a third set of notes. 'Otherwise, that branch is a dead loss. Too rough to yield prints, not that this operator would have kindly removed his gloves to leave a few prints for us to find. The lab says it could have made that bruise on her jaw, assuming it was used to shove her out into the deeper water.'

'Very good. What else?'

'The step-ladder is of no use to us. Prints belonging to François and the usual smudges. The planks are a different matter.' Kergrist picked up his remaining paper. 'They went to town on those. There is an exact match, knot for knot, in the wood, with the casts we made. And mud lodged in cracks is the same as the soil samples we took by the lake. They seem to be very pleased with what they have got out of those planks. I can't see that it does all that much for us,' he added, sourly.

'What about the other items?'

'Not ready yet. They did the most important things first. They'll phone through as soon as they have reports on the rest.'

Kergrist shuffled his papers together, then stuffed them in his pocket. 'I don't think we are going to get much more from the laboratory, Commissaire. There is no direct proof coming

173

our way. It is all circumstantial evidence. What we need is a confession.'

Orloff gazed at him. 'Am I to understand that you feel you could obtain one?'

'I would like to have a try.'

'This is your territory, Brigadier. I'm only a visitor. You must do as you think fit.'

Kergrist gave him a sharp glance. The Commissaire was the senior man, and in charge of the case under very high authority. To be retiring was also extremely out of character. He was up to one of his little games, for sure.

But he had not vetoed the idea. The Brigadier determined to press on.

'I would not care to act without your agreement, Commissaire,' he said doggedly. 'The evidence seems to me to point in one direction only. To a conspiracy between Bernard de Montigny and some other person. I do not see how he could have carried out the murder of Estelle de Saint Brieuc alone. There is no way that he could have carted all that water into the house, in advance of meeting Estelle shortly after eleven that night. We know he was in Paris, which is a long way from Brittany, until the day of her death. That morning he went by train to Morlaix to see his client, and so far we have not turned up any garage that hired a car to him. Even with transport, leaving Morlaix after nine o'clock, when Madame Beguy went to bed, he could have reached Keralic before eleven, but not early enough to organise the water, even assuming that he had a key to get into the house. He couldn't know that the door was left open for Marie-France.'

'You are building the strongest possible case for his innocence,' Orloff remarked.

'That is the whole point, Commissaire. I think de Montigny did sleep innocently in Morlaix that night and then took the train back to Paris the next day. It didn't matter where he was, as long as it could be proved that it was impossible for him to be at Keralic. The two murders must be linked, so, since he could not have killed Estelle, he is automatically ruled out for the killing of Marie-France.'

'So?' Orloff prompted, as Kergrist paused.

'It would be a two-way thing. He could not commit one murder and his partner could not commit the other. I don't believe a woman could have fixed up that trap at the grotto.'

'Personally, I was satisfied of Mademoiselle Bracebridge's innocence.'

'I am not speaking of her, Commissaire, but of the man's mother, Madame de Montigny.'

Orloff's face registered nothing but detached interest.

'I see. The motive being to gain possession of Keralic in due course, which, in view of the General's advanced age, cannot be so very long.'

'For him, yes,' said Kergrist, not looking at the Commissaire. 'For her, a very thorough revenge.' He paused, then added: 'I thought you might prefer me to handle it.'

There was a short silence, and Kergrist wondered if he had made a mistake. But Josephine de Montigny was a beautiful woman and there might be a chink in the armour of Maximilien Orloff. 'If you don't mind me mentioning it,' he muttered.

'Not at all,' said Orloff calmly. 'Madame de Montigny must be interrogated. I should be obliged if you would begin at once. I will remain here for a while. I will join you at Keralic later.'

The Quennecs were opening the shop for the day's business when their son came through from the house at the back.

'Georges!' Odile flew to him. 'How are you?'

He summoned up a smile. 'I've felt better!'

'Your head?' she enquired, anxiously.

Georges reached up to touch the sticking plaster covering the wound.

'A crack on the skull won't hurt me, Mother. It was the drink. I'll survive. Thanks for rescuing me. And thank you, Father, for taking me in.'

Jules Quennec laid down a side of beef. 'This is your home, Georges. You are welcome whenever you want to come.' He put out his hand. 'Let bygones be bygones, eh?'

'I would like that,' said Georges simply.

Father and son shook hands. Odile burst into tears.

175

'Now, Mother,' said Jules, red with embarrassment. 'What will the customers think? Some old gossip will spread the rumour that I am beating you.'

'Don't be silly?' she sniffed, wiping her eyes with the corner of her apron.

Georges gave her a quick hug.

'Mother, I don't want you to misunderstand, but I'm going to Keralic.'

'Please, Georges, don't!'

'I have to. For Estelle. After that, I promise you I will put it all behind me.'

'But what are you going to do there?'

'I don't know. Talk, if they will let me,' he said.

'I wish you wouldn't. That place only brings you bad luck. Look what happened yesterday.'

Georges laughed.

'That was nothing to do with luck. I was full of anger and I had spent a couple of hours tanking up to bolster my courage. A ditch was all I was fit for! Today is different. I am just going to say my piece and leave it at that. This isn't a perfect world. Justice doesn't always triumph. I can't make it. The Saint Brieucs are going to get away with it, thanks to the strings they can pull. But I want them to have to live with the fact that I know what they did to Estelle and Marie-France.'

'Let him go, Mother,' Jules recommended. 'He won't be satisfied until he has seen them. If he can get in, that is. They say the place is crawling with police.'

'I'll get in, never fear,' said Georges, confidently. 'There's a way in from the river, and a path from the bridge.'

Lottie and Caroline were in the drawing room. The girl stared out of the window at the bright weather and the garden emerging from the snow like an awakened sleeper shrugging off the blankets. Tears rolled silently down her cheeks.

'Must you snivel?' demanded Lottie, crossly.

'I'm sorry,' said Caroline, but the tears still came.

'You can't expect me to sympathise. Josephine has haunted me for thirty years and I have suffered agonies every time Bernard has entered this house.'

'Agonies? You, Aunt Lottie?'

'Everyone thinks I have no feelings. That is because I was brought up to show a brave face to the world. I suggest you do the same.'

'I love him!'

'You'll get over it. If Bernard killed my girls, he isn't the man you thought he was, is he?'

'I don't believe it!' said Caroline violently. 'And I can't believe it of Josephine, either.'

'The police must have found some evidence against them or they wouldn't be questioning them now. How long have they been in there?'

Caroline looked at her watch. 'Nearly an hour. I thought it was longer than that.'

Berthe came bursting in from the dining room.

'That Commissaire has just arrived. I saw him through the kitchen window.'

'Then what are you doing here?' said Lottie, but with only half of her usual venom. 'Let him in.'

Berthe shot her a mutinous look, but went to the door.

Orloff came into the room. Caroline stared at him in pure terror.

'Have you come to arrest Josephine?' Lottie demanded.

'No, Madame. I have come for Colonel Clermont. Where is he?'

Lottie gaped at him. 'Edouard? He's out in the garden somewhere. With Léon.'

The Commissaire was already throwing open the library door. He strode through, and they heard him shouting in the anteroom for Brigadier Kergrist. Then he returned to the drawing room.

'Which way have they gone, Madame?'

'I don't know,' said Lottie, bewildered.

The room was suddenly full of people: the Brigadier and a few of his men, Berthe, François the gardener, who had been enjoying a chat in the kitchen, even Josephine and Bernard, who looked more bewildered than anyone.

'Search the grounds,' Orloff commanded. 'Everyone get out there. Find the General and Colonel Clermont.' He glanced at Caroline and Bernard, clasped in each other's

177

arms. 'Break it up, you two. It's a matter of life and death.'

'Whose death?' demanded Lottie, awkward to the last, as the room emptied rapidly.

'The General's, Madame,' said Orloff, as Josephine fled into the kitchen.

The Commissaire followed her.

They were at the grotto, the two old comrades, staring at the wrecked building, as, so many times in war, they had stood in shell-shattered towns. Open now to the sky, the sun streamed in, lighting up the cascade on the rear wall, running freely now, no longer blocked by ice and snow. Outside, the water in the twin pools rippled in the breeze. Through the trees which marked the end of the garden, the river at full-tide ran silver.

'I want you to know that I am truly sorry about Marie-France,' said Edouard Clermont. 'I had no idea she and that boy met here.'

Léon roused himself from a reverie. He was thinking about Josephine and he wished Edouard would keep quiet.

'What did you say?'

'It was all to protect Michel, you know. I don't care about myself. My life is over. Estelle had got hold of your diary and she threatened to send it to a newspaper if I didn't give her half my house. I didn't mind about the house, but I couldn't trust her not to blab the whole thing to someone. I couldn't take the risk. It was not fair to Michel. The sin was mine, but it would rub off on him.'

Horror flooded over Léon. He stared at his old friend, incapable of accepting the evidence of his ears.

'My diary? Not the Indo-China one? Edouard, are you talking about the massacre?'

'I couldn't let her do it, Léon. Think what the press would have made of it.'

Now the terrible truth had to be believed. 'Dear God, Edouard!' Léon gasped. 'What have you done?'

'I am telling you, Léon. I couldn't risk exposure. For Michel's sake. It could ruin his career, being shown up as the son of a mass-murderer. All those women and children—'

'Stop it, Edouard! I am not excusing what you did, but

terrible mistakes happen in wartime. Especially in a dirty war like that.'

'It has never left me for a moment. All these years, and it's still as fresh as the day it happened. I can smell that filthy village in the jungle. And I can smell the blood!'

In the wood above them, a bird sang, a clear shining sound rising to heaven.

'You killed Estelle. You!' said Léon, in a stunned voice.

'You must see, I had to. I arranged to meet her in the flower-room. She would give me the diary. I would give her a written promise to hand over half my house to her as a wedding present. I had filled the bin with water from the lake—'

'Oh, God!' Léon groaned.

'And I couldn't let you write your memoirs, either. I thought you were the only one to visit the grotto. But it went wrong. It was like the massacre all over again when I found that poor little Marie-France had sprung the trap. I am not fit to live, Léon, but it is my duty to protect Michel. Estelle is dead. The diary is burnt. I think Commissaire Orloff knows the truth. So there is no time left. For either of us. We must go together, Léon.'

The General saw his old friend advancing upon him.

'Edouard! No! Listen to me!'

There was no reaction in the Colonel's face. He came on remorselessly and Léon had time to think that this was what those villagers saw. That set, blind face – and, for them, the machine-gun.

Then Edouard was upon him, forcing him back towards the ornamental pools. Léon fought, but the crippled limbs could not do what trained fighting instinct decreed. Together they fell and he felt the cold water in his face.

Down. Into water only a metre deep. But deep enough....

Then, suddenly, the pressure ceased. He heard a great cry and running feet as someone leapt into the pool beside him and lifted him up. He lay gasping on the patterned stone apron in front of the grotto.

'Will you be all right there?' said a voice. 'I'll go and get help.'

Léon looked up into the face of a perfect stranger, who was engaged in taking off his coat to spread it over his wet body.

'Who are you?' he panted.

A faint smile appeared on the man's face. He tucked the coat round Léon. 'Georges Quennec.'

The old man struggled up to a sitting position, pulling the welcome coat round him as shivers ran through his body.

'Well, Georges, I can't say I'm sorry that you've come to Keralic at last. Do you realise you've just saved my life? Where is Edouard?'

'The old boy who was in the water with you? He took off when I appeared. Leapt the wall like a young 'un. He'll be halfway along the path to the bridge by now.'

Léon shook his head.

'No. He's gone into the river.'

'Do you think so? I'd better go after him.'

'Let him go. It's better that way. He killed Estelle and Marie-France.'

Georges stared. 'How do you know?'

'He told me. It was something about the house. I didn't quite follow it.'

Georges groaned. 'My God! She wanted it for me. For me!'

'And Marie-France was just a terrible accident. It was meant for me.'

'You? Why?'

Léon sighed. 'He was afraid I would publish something in my memoirs. If I did, he thought it would destroy his son. As if I would! But he had passed beyond reason. He was my best friend.'

'I was wrong about you,' said Georges bleakly. 'I thought—'

'I know what you thought, my boy. It doesn't matter now. Believe it or not, Lottie and I tried to do our best for Estelle. Now, take me up to the house, there's a good fellow. I must get out of these wet clothes.'

He looked up, to see Josephine running towards him. She had not stopped for either boots or coat, and never had she appeared more beautiful.

Behind her came Commissaire Orloff. He took in the two bedraggled figures.

'Ah, yes, Madame,' he said. 'I was sure you would know where to find him.'

'You are too late,' said Georges. 'He's gone.'

'Where?'

He gestured with his arm towards the river.'

Orloff pulled a whistle from his pocket and blew one short blast. Answering shouts echoed down the valley.

Josephine knelt beside her former lover.

'You're soaked!' she exclaimed. 'And this coat is not much better,' she added, feeling the sleeves of Georges's jacket. 'What on earth have you been doing? We must get you to the house at once. Can you walk?'

Gendarmes came running, and Orloff despatched them to look for the Colonel. Then he stripped off his overcoat and handed it to Josephine.

'Wrap this round him. Let's get him up. Monsieur!' he called to Georges, who seemed to be dissociating himself from the scene, and was staring out across the river. 'Help me, please!'

The two men heaved the General to his feet, as Lottie came round the twisting path. She stopped short when she saw Josephine.

'Trust you to get to him first!' she said, then her eyes widened as she saw the water dripping from her husband. 'What has happened?'

'Edouard tried to drown me,' said Léon, in a faraway voice. 'Georges pulled me out.'

'Georges?' said Lottie, blankly, gazing at the stranger supporting Léon.

'Your butcher's boy, Madame,' Georges said, but with no bitterness now.

Lottie's face flushed scarlet.

Josephine stepped forward.

'Madame, please take the General back to the house. He is soaked to the skin.'

'Where's my stick?' Léon enquired, but it was nowhere to be seen.

Lottie bustled forward, all but pushed Orloff aside to take the General's arm.

'Come on,' she said, and looked across at Georges. 'Will you help me? He'll catch his death of cold if he stays out here much longer.'

Georges stared for a moment, then nodded, and the three of them moved slowly away down the path.

'That was graciously done, Madame,' said Orloff, as they passed out of sight, leaving him alone with Josephine.

'They have only each other now, for what life is left,' she said.

'And you?'

She smiled. 'I haven't spent the past thirty years nursing a broken heart. I thought I would, but somewhere along the way the wound healed. All that remains is pity. For both of them.'

They had assembled in the drawing room, once more, at the General's request. The old man sat huddled in a dressing-gown and blankets. The others crowded round him: Lottie, uncharacteristically protective; Caroline and Bernard, inseparable after their recent ordeal; Josephine, quiet and composed; even Georges Quennec, surprised to find himself accepted after all the harsh words of the past.

Commissaire Orloff and Brigadier Kergrist came in.

'Gentlemen,' said Léon, who appeared to be recovering rapidly. 'Please be seated. Commissaire, I know I should not ask you this, but we would be very glad of a little explanation.'

'I think you are entitled to that, General,' said Orloff, aware of Kergrist's disapproval. 'After all, there can be no prosecution. While you were making your statement, some fishermen pulled Clermont's body out of the river.'

'Poor Edouard!' said Léon. 'The last person in the world I would have suspected.'

'You had caught up with him, Commissaire,' Lottie, irrepressible as ever, interrupted. 'You came here looking for him.'

'Yes. At long last I had found a tiny bit of proof. One fingerprint, overlooked, on a bottle of preserved cherries.'

'What!' shrieked Lottie. 'Those cherries!'

'Exactly, Madame. You do the preserving yourself, I imagine. Pure alcohol, poured onto raw fruit. It makes a most potent brew, which was added to the bottle of sweet vermouth that was your daughter's habitual drink. That is confirmed by the laboratory analysis of the contents of that bottle. The idea was to make her much more drunk than she would have been on two *apéritifs* and two glasses of wine. To make her easier to overpower.'

'Then Berthe—' Lottie began, and broke off.

'Quite innocent, Madame. You will have to find something else to quarrel over. But we must all be thankful for the row over those cherries. Between us, Brigadier Kergrist and I had established how Estelle was killed, and it followed that the killer was also responsible for Marie-France's death. Yet we had no indication as to which one of you that person was. And we had come to the conclusion that we should have to interrogate you again and again, until eventually the pressure would become too great, and we should obtain a confession. As, indeed, we have, although hardly in the way we expected. And now we must go,' Orloff said smoothly. 'Poor policemen have reports to write.'

He and Kergrist had gone before the others realised that he had told them very little. Josephine ran after them, catching the Commissaire just as he was about to take his seat in the car where Kergrist was already running the engine. A curious expression crossed Orloff's face.

'Madame?'

She stopped short a few paces from him. 'Did you really think I was a murderess, even for five minutes?'

'Are you expecting an apology?'

She faced up to him, the light of battle in her eyes. 'Something like that.'

He smiled. 'Then we must talk about it – soon.'

He put out his hand, and when she took it, raised her fingers to his lips.

'Au revoir, Madame.'

'That man is a smooth talker,' said Lottie. 'I don't know if you noticed, but he told us next to nothing. So our oldest friend turns out to be a murderer and is caught by a bottle of cherries, of all things! Léon, is that true?'

The General sighed.

'That Edouard killed our girls? Yes, I'm afraid that he did. He told me.'

'But why?'

'Estelle was blackmailing him to provide a roof for herself and Georges. Marie-France was a mistake. The trap was set for me. It was the memoirs that started it all. If those diaries had stayed at the back of a cupboard, Estelle would never have found out about the massacre.'

'What massacre?' demanded Bernard, beating Lottie by a short head.

The door opened and Josephine slipped into the room. Her son, sitting in a position to command the best view of that end of the room, was astonished to see the expression on her face: the cat with the cream, no less.

'What massacre?' he repeated.

The General passed a weary hand over his face. 'These things happen in war,' he said heavily. 'I must ask all of you never to speak of this outside this room. Michel Clermont is my godson, and he has a great future before him. Broadcasting the truth can't bring back my girls, and might ruin him. I have your promise?'

There was a general murmur of consent.

'There is no written record of the massacres now. I wish to God I had never even put a note about it in my diary! It happened in a little village in a clearing in the jungle in Indo-China. There was an ambush, and Edouard lost over three hundred men. I wasn't there, but I questioned all the witnesses. The whole battalion was raging. A few days later, they retook the village. The people pleaded innocence, of course, snickering behind their fingers at having lured so many Frenchmen to their deaths. In a blind rage, Edouard snatched up a machinegun and wiped out the lot of them, men, women and children. And every man with him cheered him to the echo. I had to put the lid on it. It was made perfectly clear to me that the troops would mutiny if I took any official action against their colonel. Edouard was a good soldier, with a fine record behind him. He agreed to resign his commission as soon as decently possible. So it was left at that. You may feel that I made the wrong decision. Certainly I have paid for it now. But at the time, it seemed to be the only

184

thing to do. The war was in a critical stage, and we were in enough trouble without a mutiny to add to it. We were in a beleaguered position. The enemy would have been on us the moment there was any dissension within our own ranks. So I weighed the lives of my men against those of the villagers. I'm sorry, Lottie. I had no idea what I would be doing to you.'

For once, she had nothing to say.

Brigadier Kergrist drove through the gates of Keralic.

'You got out of that one rather smartly, Commissaire,' he said grudgingly. 'I thought we would be there for hours.' He paused, then added: 'You saved my face, too, over having a go at Madame de Montigny and her son.'

Orloff glanced at him. The Brigadier's expression was set. 'You think I made a monkey out of you.'

Kergrist said nothing, since that was exactly what was in his head.

'I didn't want to move against Clermont until I had everything the lab could give me,' Orloff explained. 'He hadn't made a slip of any sort, and I was hoping against hope that the last items – the cherries and the Martini bottle were all that was outstanding – might give me the break I needed. At the same time, I didn't want him to have the smallest hint that I was onto him. I was afraid it would provoke an immediate attack on the General. Your descent upon the de Montigny's was the ideal screen for my activities.'

'Glad to have been of service,' said Kergrist, with a sigh.

'I wasn't quite as clever as I thought. The General tells me that Clermont knew I was after him. I don't know how. Perhaps it was bad conscience. The Colonel had been a brave soldier and an honourable man.'

'I doubt if I would have got to him,' said the Brigadier. 'How did you do it?'

'Through my silly little details, as usual.'

'Which I missed. Those cherries, for instance.'

'I was looking for something that would make Estelle drunk. The drinks she had with the others weren't enough to account for her condition. Her mother insisted that she had a bottle in her room. There wasn't one. I put aside the theory that someone had removed that bottle and worked from the

185

idea that there never had been a bottle in Estelle's bedroom. So I was looking for something to add to a bottle of sweet vermouth. And there were those two old women battling about cherries preserved in alcohol.'

'I'm glad that bottle of whisky was a fairy story,' said Kergrist. 'I didn't like to think that one of my men had helped himself to it. But those cherries can't have led you to Clermont. Anyone in the house could have done that.'

'It was the grotto. Clermont had been a demolition expert. Who was more likely to know how a roof would fall?'

'That stuck out a mile. It was no secret. But it was too obvious. And he had no visible motive for killing Marie-France.'

'That was enough to put anyone off,' said Orloff.

'Not you, Commissaire.'

'I have a devious turn of mind. Marie-France was not the only regular visitor to the grotto. The General had been going there for thirty years. And since he had come to Keralic, Clermont had accompanied his host on the daily walk. So if it had gone according to plan he would have been there when the roof collapsed, to remove the rope and the nail, and, I imagine, to make sure that the General was dead. With that vault known to be in a bad condition, no one would have suspected anything but a tragic accident. It must have been a terrible shock for Clermont when Marie-France was killed by his booby-trap. He was a newcomer to the household and I doubt if he was much interested in Marie-France or she in him. He couldn't know that she met Chester Roach at the grotto.'

Orloff broke off as a small car came rocketing round a bend, in the middle of the road. Kergrist swerved, and muttered a curse. Narrowly, they missed the ditch where Georges Quennec had fallen.

'Back to normal, now the snow has gone,' said Kergrist. 'Go on, Commissaire. What else?'

'The house Estelle was obtaining interested me. She was definite about it in her letter to Georges. The matter was on the point of being settled. Yet no one knew anything of it, nor were there any papers in her possession which related to it. Furthermore, she was not asking her mother to pay for it.

186

What she was hoping to get from her mother was an income. So how was she getting hold of the house? And there was the Colonel, her godfather, with a big house in the south of France. Yet there was nothing out in the open, so she was not throwing herself upon his charity. If she was blackmailing her mother, she could be playing the same game with the old man. So I looked round for a hint of anything she might be holding over him that was serious enough to lead to murder.'

'The missing diary,' said Kergrist, pulling up at the traffic lights at the end of the bridge.

'It wasn't much of a clue, but there was nothing else. If the diary interested anyone in the house, it had to be Clermont. It related to the war in Indo-China. The significant fact is that Clermont threw up his army career as soon as he came home from there. It struck me that the two things might be connected.'

The lights changed to green and they moved off.

'The General was not very forthcoming about that, beyond admitting that Clermont had been involved in an incident and had been allowed to retire afterwards,' Kergrist remarked. 'Frankly, I didn't believe him when he said his memory was failing.'

'Neither did I. I suspect he, too, was trying to protect Clermont's son. Very generous of him!'

Kergrist pulled into the yard in front of the Gendarmerie. Tremerrec was going about its normal business: he recognised a few of the cars parked there, and knew he was in for another busy day; an old woman waddled up the steps on her way to lay her regular complaint about her neighbour's dog; a fat habitual drunk elbowed his way through the double doors on his way out after a night in the cells; the cathedral carillon ushered in another hour.

'How are you going back to Paris, Commissaire? By train, or will they send a chopper for you?'

'Monsieur le Ministre Michel Clermont is not going to be very pleased with me. There is some leave due to me, so I don't think I'll show my face in Paris for a couple of days. I'll give him time to get used to the situation. I think I'll hire a car and spend a little time at Lazardrieux,' said Orloff blandly.

'It's the wrong time of the year for sightseeing.'

187

'I have something in mind to amuse myself,' said the Commissaire.

That evening, Caroline came down early to the drawing room. Lottie was there before her.

She gazed resentfully at her great-niece.

'I suppose there is nothing I can say to stop you marrying Bernard.'

'That's right,' said Caroline, squaring up for battle.

But, amazingly, Lottie was ready for a truce.

'You will need money to keep up this place, after we have gone. I will settle some on you.'

Caroline gaped at her. 'That is very good of you,' she stammered.

'I don't want that creature your father has married spending it all,' Lottie returned, brushing aside all thanks.

Bernard came in and was suitably stunned by the news.

'I don't know what to say,' he admitted, at a loss for once in his life.

'There is no need to say anything. Damn you, but you are the image of your father!' Lottie said gruffly, and turned away to hide some emotion.

Josephine burst into the room, her coat over her arm and looking like a million dollars.

'Bernard! I was looking for you. May I borrow your car?'

He looked her over. 'Where are you going?' he demanded, suspiciously.

'I'm having dinner with Maximilien Orloff. I can take a taxi if you don't trust me with your car.'

'No!' he exploded. 'At least with my car you'll be obliged to come back!' He fished the keys out of his pocket and handed them to her. 'Don't forget you're coming to Paris with me tomorrow.'

Josephine laughed. 'I wouldn't count on it.'

'I hope you know what you are doing,' Bernard said, thunderstruck.

'It is a long time since I had an adventure. I rather fancy this one,' she said and swept out of the room.